TRANCER

Darryl Sollerh

A Novella

TRANCER

TRANCER

A freezing chill grips Kunduz Provence, Afghanistan, holding it hostage to the night as an uneasy silence crouches in the shadows, bracing as if for an imminent onslaught.

A moment later, it arrives.

Tracer rounds suddenly flash out of the dark, streaking across a hilly pass like phosphorescent arrows as mortars plummet out in the black sky, exploding in concussive bursts that boil up into scorching fireballs.

Out of the chaos a man in robes comes running, desperately trying to escape this hell.

Scrambling over the rocky terrain, he trips and stumbles to his knees, but regains his footing to press on in the pitch black, desperately trying to flee the battle, the war, the curse on this land.

Arriving at a ravine, he slides down into its protective crevice to hurry on, making his way to safety, only to be jettisoned by a last second explosion that tosses him up like a rag doll and then tumbles him back to earth, face first into the dirt.

Unable to move, he lays there, his ears ringing, his eyes burning, his head pounding as a small, quiet thought circles his mind:

I love my country.
I believe in my country.
I would die for my country.
I just don't know which country is my country.

~*~

Under a glaring New Mexico sun, a lone highway stretches out like a desiccated snakeskin, pulled across endless, nameless miles of browning saguaros, parched pig-weed and dry desert scrub.

In the distance, riding its singed surface, a rippling black dot shimmers into view, shape-shifting in the undulating heat-waves to congeal into a black, government-issue Ford SUV approaching at a fast clip.

In it, CIA Assistant Secretary to the director Ackerman, a sixties career man with a youthful enthusiasm for his work, watches with fascination as the arid terrain whips past his window. Across from him, his late-twenties attaché, a young man with a Georgetown degree, winces, preferring the infinitely more civilized comforts of air conditioning to the ravages of desert life.

As they advance, they can see a sun-baked warehouse ahead, apparently abandoned, but still guarded by a corroding chain link fence.

The SUV slows, drawing down to ease onto the highway's shoulder, kicking up dust devils as it brakes, turns and pulls up to the entrance gate where a small, camouflaged security camera discreetly tilts to inspect it.

A moment later, the gate opens as if by magic.

The SUV drives in and continues around to the back of the warehouse, out of the highway's view, where a loading bay door opens like a mouth.

Striding down a dim hallway, Ackerman makes his way to an unmarked door, flanked by his attaché.

Emily Pinder, a research specialist in her thirties, already gaining a reputation for her tireless work, steps from her office, lost in thought. But the instant she sees Ackerman her eyes fire to life:

Secretary Ackerman?

His attaché indicates 'not now' as Ackerman enters the unmarked door, all business.

Once inside, Ackerman and attaché take up seats to peer through a two-way mirror into what looks like a Middle-Eastern hospital patient's room, replete with its stucco-walls, pastel turquoise hues and dated medical devices.

The patient, Gavin Chance, a young, Louisiana-bred recruit of mixed blood, is laying on a hospital bed as a physician, a gentle Middle-Eastern doctor, pastes diodes onto Chance's shaved head.

Apparently unaware he's being observed, or that this has all been staged, Chance confides in his doctor, revealing the defining moment of his life:

So that by the time I came to, our truck was already up in flames. I tried ta get ta her, ta save her, but...

Chance's eyes mist at the memory as his doctor regards him compassionately:

When was this?

Chance has to think, strangely unsure:

…Year before last?

About the time you volunteered?

'Recruiter said it'd be like takin' a mental vacation from everythin', which sounded pretty good ta me.

His doctor nods understandingly and pastes the last diode into place:

So I take this is your first time away from home?

Yes, sir.

So what do you think?

Chance considers it and then replies:

All in all, think I prefer home, sir.

His doctor smiles, gets up and moves to an aging laptop to type in some instructions as Chance looks on apprehensively.

Okay, we're set, Chance. You ready?

Chance draws in a deep breath, exhales and then nods, bracing himself as his doctor adds:

Just try to relax, okay? In three, two...

Chance's body suddenly jolts up with the surge of energy, only to quickly collapse again onto his bed, unconscious.

In the adjoining room, Ackerman arches a concerned brow as the doctor clicks another key, triggering a nearby monitor to display a rush of images depicting Afghan tribal life.

As they blur across its screen, the doctor moves to check Chance's vitals, beaming a flashlight into his pupils, and then timing Chance's pulse.

Satisfied, he steps back to his laptop and clicks another key, shutting down the program.

As the monitor screen goes dark, Ackerman leans forward, wholly focused on Chance who is drifting slowly back into consciousness as if from a deep, otherworldly dream, only to get filled with sudden alarm when he opens his eyes.

He sits up, panicked, and blurts out in Pashtu:

Where am I? Who are you?

His doctor calmly answers him in Pashtu:

My name is Dr. Ahmed, and you are in Jalalabad Hospital.

3

Chance looks around, trying to get his bearings as Ahmed continues:

You took a bad fall, my friend, but you'll be fine....What's your name?

Chance has to think before responding:

Masood.

His doctor nods:

Allahu Akbar, Masood.

Chance responds, easing:

...Allahu Akbar.

In the observation room, Ackerman shoots an electric look to his attaché as his doctor helps Chance – now 'Masood' – sit up in bed:

We should have you back to your village, and your life, in a matter of days.

Masood nods, feeling the urgency:

Yes. It's planting season, so I need to get back.

Moments later, Ackerman and attaché burst from the room and stride back up the hallway, invigorated.

Emily, waiting for them, hurries after them:

Mr. Secretary? Mr. Secretary, sir?

Ackerman turns to find Emily catching up, extending her hand:

Emily Pinder, sir.

Ackerman eyes her, putting a face to the name:

Ah yes, Ms. Pinder. Very impressive work.

He shakes her hand warmly.

Thank you, sir. And I was wondering if you received my transfer request?

Ackerman nods:

Yes. Indeed I did. Remind me Ms. Pinder: how long have you been on this project?

Just under five years, sir, which is why I'm hoping you'll grant my transfer.

Ackerman eyes her more carefully:

You're sure you want to work in the field?

Yes, sir.

Ackerman glances at his attaché and then looks back to Emily:

4

Field work can be extremely dangerous, Ms. Pinder. Are you absolutely sure that's what you want?

Yes, sir. Very sure.

Ackerman thinks about it and then says:

In that case, given what I just witnessed, consider your request granted.

As Ackerman and his attaché move on, Emily fist-pumps the air and, for lack of someone to share this victory with, chest-thumps the wall, living out yet one more of her life-defining moments alone.

Stepping back into her tiny, cramped office, she looks around, still marveling that her wish was granted, gradually sobering at what it will mean.

A week later, Emily finds herself hustling across an army base airfield, toting her equipment to an impossibly huge Boeing C-17 Globemaster Transport plane as Ackerman's voice echoes in her head: *You will embed with Special Forces in Kunduz province to assist in T Tech operations...*

As she boards the B-17, stepping into its immense cargo bay, she can hear and feel its four engines thundering to life, shaking the plane.

Finding a seat, she starts buckling herself in as a crewman passes by, checking a passenger manifest, and yells:

You Pinder?

Yes.

He looks her over, straining to hear:

You're not Army, are you?

She calls back:

Consultant.

The Crewman smirks, pegging her for a profiteer:

Defense contractor. Well, that's where the money is!

That's not why I—

But the B-17 lurches into motion, compelling the crewman to move off as the plane rumbles forward as it taxis onto the runway.

Moments later, its engines roar again, accelerating the plane into frenzy before finally lifting it into flight. Emily watches the Army base and then the earth, drop away from view, and for a moment she feels almost like a departing soul, overjoyed at its sudden liberation from the world, but quickly growing concerned by the uncertain afterlife lying in wait.

~*~

Kunduz Province. Dead of night.

Four men hide in the shadows of a rocky pass, their heads wrapped in Shemagh head scarves, their bodies cloaked in tribal robes, their faces greased, their hands cradling M4A1 rifles as they spy down on the temporary encampment of three Afghan tribesmen.

But rival tribesmen they are not.

They are rather a US Special Forces team doing the covert work of war, even if America's official involvement has ended.

Brody, a blonde, late twenties second lieutenant, receives a Satcom message in his ear-bud and leans over to whisper to Kraig, his Captain, a seasoned warrior in his late thirties with darkening eyes.

Satellite's picking up Hadj movements 1 tick north.

Craig smirks:

Hunting us, no doubt.

Kraig checks the time:

Let's get this done.

Kraig peers into his night-vision scope to see a green-hued view of the three Afghan fighters bedding down for the night.

As one of the fighters lingers outside the tent to finish his cigarette, Kraig takes out another high-tech scope and peers through that and sees a faint, red signal emanating from the smoking fighter's torso.

Brody looks to Kraig:

That him?

Kraig nods and signals to Sconstantly and Riggs, crouching behind.

Sealar and Riggs nod back, signaling they're ready to go.

So Kraig takes out a small, remote device – something akin to a garage door opener – and, glancing around at his men one last time, clicks it.

The smoking fighter suddenly doubles over, incapacitated as if he's just been kicked in the gut. Kraig then gives the 'go' sign and his team moves out, shedding their robes to reveal their trim, equipped, black op fatigues.

They angle deftly down to the campsite, moving like phantoms in the night, in total mission control, drawing nearer and nearer, until...*Kaboom!*

An explosion suddenly sends them all flying, diving for cover as the pssft-pssft-pssft of automatic weapons fire crackles to life, blistering the ground like killer firecrackers as the team crashes back to earth.

Rocked and disoriented, their training takes over as they instinctively look to determine the angle of the attack as they scramble for cover.

Finding a jut of rocks, they dive for cover. But Kraig sees Seally still lying out in the open, exposed to the relentless barrage, so he shimmies back to him on his elbows, grabs hold of Seally under fire and drags him behind the rocks where Brody and Riggs are already returning fire.

Brody then spots the smoking fighter, the object of this mission, rallying to pick up a rifle to fire on them at close range, compelling Brody to take special aim and fire, killing the fighter instantly as another mortar round explodes near the team, forcing them to hunker down under a hail-storm of falling rocks and dust.

Kraig signals 'retreat' and the team pulls back, obscured by the dust, laying down cover fire as they withdraw back into the shadows of the mountain pass.

Moments later, on the move, Riggs takes the lead as Kraig carries Seally on his shoulder while Brody keeps watch over their wake.

As they climb higher into the mountains, hunted and pursued by their fleet-footed attackers, Riggs spots a thicket of bushes and heads for it.

There they find an overgrown creek bed and quickly slide down under the overgrowth to hide in its shallow canal, hidden by the foliage.

Riggs quickly takes up a defensive position as Kraig and Brody maneuver to perform CPR on Seally, but is forced to halt and hunker down as a band of Hakani fighters rush up, only steps from them, to confer.

The team holds its collective breath, only a few feet from certain death when the Hakanis rush off again into the night, none the wiser.

Later, half past midnight, as a slim moon arcs over a hidden mountain cave, Emily, dressed in her own black fatigues, climbs from its mouth to peer through a pair of night-vision goggles, scanning the mountain terrain until she spots the team making its way back with Kraig carrying Seally as Brody takes point and Riggs guards their wake.

She sobers, confused and alarmed as they make their way up to her:

What happened?

Kraig moves past her without a word and goes into the cave.

She watches Seally pass by on Kraig's shoulder, and can't help but respond:

Jesus.

She then looks to Brody for an explanation, but he just shakes his head and moves past her.

So she turns to Riggs, bringing up the rear:

What happened?

Riggs slows to eye her grimly:

Walked right into their kill box.

I don't understand.

He shoots her a knowing look:

They knew we were coming.

He continues on into the cave and Emily follows, even more alarmed.

Inside its rock walls, she finds Brody helping Kraig fit Seally's corpse into a body bag and asks:

But...how could they possibly know you were coming?

Kraig shakes his head, avoiding even looking at her:

Because your boy was their bait.

Despite Seally, Emily can't allow that to stand:

No. Not possible.

Brody and Riggs glance her way and then at their captain, anticipating a brawl as Kraig, livid, finally looks up:

They knew exactly where we'd be, and exactly when we'd be there.

Emily shrugs dismissively, undaunted:

He was deployed three months ago. How could he have possibly known anything about when or where you'd be coming for him, much less that anybody was coming to extract him?

Kraig has to strain hard not to explode, and looks down again at Seally, refocusing to mutter a prayer, and say a silent goodbye.

As much as Emily wants to have this out now, she bites her tongue, respecting the moment as Kraig summarily zips up Seally's body bag, stands up and heads off to the back of the cave where the communications equipment is staged.

Brody follows him, so Emily turns once more to Riggs:

So where is he?

Riggs shakes his head.

Your Trancer? He left us no choice.

Emily feels a surge of outrage shoot through her, but she contains it to counter:

Which is why you were supposed to extract him, so that I could de-trance him.

Riggs shrugs, battle-weary:

He fired on us, 'cause in his head, thanks to T Tech, he thought we were the enemy.

With that Riggs moves off to join Kraig and Brody.

She's about to follow him, to defend T-Tech – to defend herself – but she thinks better and resists the impulse, only to find herself alone with Seally.

As she eyes the body bag, beginning to absorb his loss, she finds her thoughts returning to another loss, the one that compelled her to come here in the first place. And for a moment she falters, needing the cave's wall for support.

Riggs meanwhile arrives to find Kraig finishing a call to Command via the Satcom radio:

Roger that. Pride Five out.

They both wait expectantly as Kraig turns incredulously to face them:

They're sending another.

Brody grimaces:

Another Trancer? What the...? When?

Kraig shakes his head, stupefied:

Already on his way.

A Nighthawk chopper's rotors plow the midnight air, sending thumping shock waves through its cabin as Chance, its lone passenger, stares out into the pitch black of the Afghan night – his eyes blood-shot, his mind wondering where he is, and who he is.

He checks his gear, sees the 'Cpl Bales' tag and a US flag insignia patch.

He then looks around at the pilots to note the US flag patches on their uniforms and concludes:

They seem to know me. I must be one of them.

He then notes a US flag decal on the chopper's hull, and, concerned he'll forget, takes out his knife to carve 'US' onto his inner arm, only to hear:

Going dark in 3...2...

The Nighthawk's lights shut off. Everything goes instantly dark, forcing Chance to give up his skin carving and re-sheath his knife in the darkness all around him.

An hour later, the Nighthawk blows up a dust storm as it touches down on a barren, mountain plateau.

The co-pilot cranes his neck to announce:

This is you, buddy. Good luck.

Chance quickly unbuckles, grabs his pack and slides out of the chopper bed to jump down onto the plateau's gravel surface.

Gaining his footing, he sees Brody and Riggs emerging from the shadows to lift Seally's body bag onto the chopper.

Without a word to Chance, they strap Seally down and then Brody slaps the Nighthawk's hull, signaling the pilots.

As the chopper lifts away again into the night, Brody motions to Chance to follow, and they set off into what's left of this Afghan night.

Chance follows Brody and Riggs back to the cave over the rough, cold mountain terrain, taking cover whenever Brody shunts up a 'halt' fist to check their surroundings.

He then silently leads them onwards.

Finally arriving back at the cave as dawn breaks over the peaks, Brody leads Chance in to find Kraig, who looks from cleaning his M4A1 rifle.

Corporal Bales, reporting, sir.

Kraig eyes him neutrally as Emily walks up eagerly to welcome him:

Corporal? I'm Emily Pinder, Special Consultant.

She shakes his hand as if he might recognize her, but he doesn't:

Would you come with me, please?

Confused by Kraig's unwelcoming gaze, he gladly moves off with Emily, following her back to the T Tech equipment, stacked in a corner of the cave:

Any idea where you are?

I'm guessin' pretty far from the nearest gas station?

She smiles:

Do you know why you're here?

Chance shrugs:

I lost a bet?

She has to chuckle as she offers him a seat:

We've actually worked together before.

Chance eyes her, lost.

In the New Mexico desert? Little over a year ago?

Chance looks a little embarrassed as he sinks into the seat:

Sorry. But... It's not you.

Meaning?

He becomes self-conscious, and tries to hide just how much his lack of recall scares him.

I don't seem to remember much lately.

What do you mean?

Chance demurs, reluctant to explore it. So she tries a different tactic:

When was your last deployment?

He shakes his head, unsure.

Okay, what did you do last week?

He hesitates, becoming increasingly uncomfortable.

How about yesterday?

His confusion gives way to fear, and he looks down, perplexed and scared as Emily is filled with concern; but she tries to reassure him:

It's really okay. Short-term memory loss is to be expected, and it's usually only temporary.

Chance displays a funny look. So she inquires further:

What?

It's not just short-term, ma'am.

Emily sits beside him, trying to put him at ease.

How about we set all that stuff aside, and you just tell me what you do remember.

Like what, exactly?

Like, say, where you're from? Or you could tell about your family.

He eyes her, trying to hold back an avalanche of emotions.

She senses his growing struggle:

I want you to know, Corporal Bales, that I'm here to help. Understand? In fact, you guys are the reason I'm here.

He nods, trying to look appreciative.

She gets up, retrieves a laptop and settles down beside him again to tap a computer key, bringing up his file, which she then shows him:

You grew up in Macon, Georgia. You have a sister, but your mom passed away a few years back in a car accident.

Emily watches as he eyes the screen, appraising it as if it was someone else's life. So she withdraws the laptop, pretending she needs it:

Would you excuse me for a moment, Corporal?

Emily walks up just as Kraig and Brody are finishing packing their gear for a long trek, prompting Kraig to ask before she can speak:

How soon will he be ready?

Six months. A year. Maybe never.

Kraig is forced to look up:

What are you talking about?

He's shifting.

'Shifting'?

His brain isn't able to synch with its own memory nodes.

Kraig looks to Brody and then back to Emily:

Meaning what?

Meaning that as of this moment, the corporal doesn't have a clue who he is.

Kraig's eyes narrow at her:

Thought that was the whole point of T Tech?

Emily controls herself:

No, the point of T Tech is that he always knows who he is, or at least thinks he knows who he is – even if who he thinks he is, is not who he really is.

Kraig shares another dark, dubious look with Brody as Emily continues:

The point being, Captain, he's not ready to be deployed.

Kraig takes a moment to consider it and then flatly balks:

Not my problem.

Emily tenses:

Excuse me?

Kraig gets back to his packing:

You heard me, Pinder.

Yes, I did. So perhaps I didn't make myself clear.

Kraig stops her:

Actually, you made yourself perfectly clear.

Emily, incredulous, tries another track:

Then perhaps you didn't understand what I said.

No, Pinder, it's you who don't understand. Our orders are to deploy him, so that's what we're going to do.

Even if he's not ready?

Kraig winces with disgust:

It's T Tech that isn't ready.

Emily's blood is reaching a boil, but it's only sharpening her mind:

Again, wrong. Because it's already proven itself many times over.

Kraig climbs to his feet, only too ready to have this out:

Far as I'm concerned, all it's 'proven' is that it can cause two men to die for no damn good reason!

Emily grimaces:

If that's what you think, then how's deploying a third man going to help?

Kraig's eyes burn as he takes a moment, considering how to respond, and then responds:

Case you hadn't noticed, Command isn't interested in what we think when it comes to T Tech, much less the 'mission readiness' of the newbies they send us to deploy.

Emily tries to use that:

Fine, then I'll speak with Command.

You do that.

As she turns to go, she hears him add:

For all the good it will do.

She stops. Turns:

What is your problem?

He shakes his head, his eyes darkened by what he's seen of this world:

Want to know how this works? Once some BS program like yours gets going, it doesn't stop. No, it just keeps going and going, and we keep sending those lambs to the slaughter you call 'Trancers' out into the filed until enough of them fail or die to where somebody up the command chain suddenly notices the casualty figures while sipping his morning coffee and calls for an investigation. Now if you'll excuse me, I have a mission to prepare for.

Her eyes burn at him as he refocuses on his supply pack.

She finally turns and heads off, as Brody looks over at Kraig with a wry glint:

Sure gotta way with the ladies, bro.

Moments later, Emily makes her appeal to Command via the Satcom, only to be cut quickly back down to size:

But he can't even recall his... Yes, sir.

She clicks off, stricken. She looks back in Kraig's direction, secretly worried Kraig's right, but then she tries to regroup for Chance's benefit.

That evening, she finds herself pasting a select few diodes behind his ear as he looks to her for reassurance:

So will my memories ever come back?

After your deployment, I promise I will do everything I can to help you get them back. All right?

Chance nods, but he does so for her benefit and not because he believes her.

She checks the diode connections and then restrains his hands with a plastic tie fastener, just as if he was a prisoner. He allows it, resigned to his fate. But he then suddenly looks to her:

I just...

She waits, anxious to hear whatever he needs to say:

...You just 'what', corporal?

What I'm doin', this mission, even if I can't remember stuff, it helps, right?

Emily grits her teeth, biting back tears.

It helps very much. In fact it saves lives.

Relieved, he nods, satisfied, now ready to endure anything.

So Emily, feeling ever more conflicted, gets up and moves to her laptop, looks at him once more, and then finally taps the requisite key.

The Afghan mountains. Hakani territory. 2am.

Kraig, Brody and Riggs lead a hooded and handcuffed Chance, now dressed in traditional Afghan robes, towards two huts of a mountainside date farm.

Stopping short, they lower Chance onto his knees.

As Brody and Riggs move off, their breath fogging the chilling night air, Kraig strikes Chance's hooded head with his rifle butt.

As Chance slumps over, shocked and dazed, Kraig removes the hood and, taking it with him, hustles back into the darkness to join Brody and Riggs, hiding nearby.

Kraig then takes out a 'soflam' laser and points its invisible beam at a nearby hillside. Then he nods to Brody, who whispers into the mobile Satcom receiver...

Moments later, a Hellfire missile streaks down from an unseen drone in the black sky to explode violently into a hillside, its boom echoing out into the mountains.

Kraig grabs his night-vision goggles and peers back at Chance to see him groping back to consciousness, climbing unsteadily back to his feet to look around, confused.

When he spots the two huts, he starts towards them, and Kraig signals the team, prompting them to silently withdraw into the night.

As Chance nears the huts, still walking unsteadily, he hears a gruff voice shout 'Stop!' in Pashtu.

He turns cautiously to see Tariq, a man with scorpion eyes, stepping from behind a tree, training a Kalashnikov rifle on him:

Who are you?...Answer me.

Chance wants to answer – even tries to – but then falls forward in a faint.

Minutes later, entering one of the huts, Tariq, carrying Chance over his shoulder, dumps him onto its floor as Nadjia, all but hidden under her hijab, arrives, startled from her sleep.

She takes one look at Chance's bleeding head and moves off to get what first aid she can offer.

Tariq meanwhile scavenges Chance's pockets, disgusted to find nothing of value.

Nadjia returns with water and a cloth, and indicates that Tariq should move aside. Then she kneels beside Chance to attend to his wounds, avoiding eye contact.

Tariq scowls as he watches her gently dab at Chance's bleeding wounds, just as Chance begins to wheeze back to life.

Nadjia repositions herself to help Chance sit upright so that he can catch his breath. As she does, Tariq's eyes burn to life and he shoves her back indignantly:

You touch him?

But he cannot breathe!

Chance, now gasping as he fights for air, instinctively, if weakly, tries to intercede on Nadjia's behalf, at which Tariq shoves his rifle's barrel onto Chance's forehead, and drives him back down onto the mat:

Down, Dog!

As Chance coughs violently, struggling desperately for air, Nadjia glares at Tariq:

He will die!

So let him.

As Tariq sniffs, relishing his power, Chance begins to turn blue, wheezing for air. So Nadjia tries a gentle approach:

Please, Tariq.

No!

Chance claws at the walls, trying to pull himself up.

Nadjia can't take it and surges forward to help. And as Tariq tries to stop her, they hear:

What is this? What's going on?

They turn to see Zerak, Nadjia's father, now in his seventies, entering, roused from his bed:

What are you doing?

She let him touch her!

No, father! I was only trying to help him sit up so that he can breathe.

Zerak, still very much in command of his affairs, moves closer to inspect Chance, motioning Tariq aside as Nadjia continues:

He needs to sit up.

Agreeing with her, Zerak himself helps Chance sit up.

As Chance coughs back to life, Zerak eyes him carefully:

Who are you?

As Chance's breathing opens up, he's able to speak:

…Masood.

Masood from where?

Of the Mezi.

Tariq glowers:

I knew it! He's a Mezi spy!

Zerak gives Tariq an impatient glare, shutting him up, and then turns back to Chance:

What are you doing so far from home, Masood?

I…

Chance struggles to recall, but can't.

…Don't know.

Tariq gesticulates:

He is a Mezi liar!
Zerak admonishes:
Enough!
Zerak then moves to check Chance's wounds and then
turns to Nadjia:
*He must have been too near to that missile. Or maybe he
was its target.*
Tariq tries to re-frame his earlier reaction as rational:
*If the Americans are after him, and he stays here, they will
send their missiles down on us!*
Zerak considers Tariq's point. He then looks back at
Chance:
Are the Americans after you?
No.
Tariq spits:
Would a Mezi liar tell us if they were?
Zerak considers the situation, weighing Chance's injuries
and the danger he may pose, and then turns to address Chance
one last time:
For now, you may rest here.
Zerak calls to the night:
Deqan?
A moment later, Deqan, Nadjia's younger brother, arrives at
the hut's door:
I want you to watch our guest.
Zerak then looks to Tariq, offering him a face-saving exit:
So you can get some rest.
Tariq stiffens:
But I am not tired.
Zerak insists:
Rest, Tariq. Every man needs his rest.
Tariq reluctantly leaves, handing Deqan the rifle as he
shoots Chance a dark glare out of Zerak's view. Zerak meanwhile
turns to Nadjia:
If he needs to move, Deqan will move him. Not you.
Yes, father.
Zerak nods and leaves.

As Nadjia rises to go, Chance tries to thank her, but she again avoids any eye contact and departs, leaving Deqan fingering the rifle's trigger in her wake.

So Chance – Masood – huddles into a corner, trying to insulate himself against the biting chill of night as Deqan keeps vigil, accustomed to the cold.

As Kraig, Brody and Riggs make their way back to the cave, traversing miles of rocky terrain in the dead of night, Brody spots the needle-like red beam of a laser rifle-site flash in the darkness and instantly reacts:

Captain!

Kraig turns, sees it too and signals for the team to take cover.

They immediately hunker down as best they can.

Kraig waits, on edge, ready to do battle.

But he then sees the laser's red dot dance onto his chest, and he lunges aside, certain he's being targeted, only to hear:

Hooya!

Kraig, face down in the dirt, scowls, filling with anger as the voice continues:

You dudes are so toast!

Kraig climbs to his feet, smoldering to see Captain Jay Price sauntering up, grinning, his thirties features smeared in camouflage grease, flanked by a first lieutenant in his twenties.

Well, if it isn't Captain DoRight and his merry band of dead-meat targets!

Kraig glares:

You kidding me, Price?

Price balks:

Would you relax, Kraig? Hell, if we can't have a little fun out here, what the hell's the point?

But Kraig's not smiling:

Don't you ever – ever – pull that again, you understand?

Price teases:

Whoa, touchy. Didn't mean to upset ya there, bro.

Price's first lieutenant snickers as Price continues:

But then, you kinda upset me first.

I upset you?

By releasin' a towel-head back into the wilds of my sector without so much as a heads-up. What the shit was that, bro?

If you got a problem, Price, talk to Command.

Yeah, 'cause they always tell us what's goin' down, dude!

They trade a knowing look, but then Kraig cuts it short:

See ya around, Price.

As Kraig and his team start off again, Price sneers:

You're some kinda boy scout, aren't ya, Kraig?

Kraig stops, turns back to Price as Price finally makes his point:

But just so we understand each other, anything that happens in this sector is my goddamn business, Kraig.

Kraig shakes his head, bemused:

'Your Sector'? What are you, the town Sheriff?

Got that right, bro.

Tell ya what, Price: you follow your orders; I'll follow mine.

As Kraig signals his team to move on, Price counters:

So what, we're like we're on different sides now, is that it?

Kraig turns back one last time, grimacing:

Really?

Price sneers:

What you don't seem to understand is that there's 'us' – the good guys – and there's 'them' – the bad guys. So instead of copping a 'tude, maybe you should be thanking your lucky stars it was us 'good guys' who had your sorry asses in our sites just now, and not them.

Kraig glances heavenward and then back at Price:

Yeah? Well what if us 'good guys' had opened up on your sorry asses the moment you tagged us with your lasers? How 'lucky' would that have been?

Naw. You're too much of a Boy Scout for that, Kraig.

Kraig, biting his tongue, heads on his way, joined by his team as Price calls sarcastically after them:

No hard feelings, Dudley.

As they move out of earshot, Brody whispers to Kraig:

I take it he hasn't been briefed?

Kraig's eyes roll:

Briefed on T Tech? Price? No goddamn way.

Back in the base cave, as Emily lies on her bedroll working her thoughts, she hears the team returning and rallies to confront Kraig.

As he un-shoulders his weapon, Emily steps forward, expecting a mission status update. Kraig notes her eager presence and offers only:

He's deployed.

As Kraig moves to attend to his gear, she continues to stand there. He finally turns:

What?

You still don't know what it is I do, do you?

He stares at her for a moment and says:

What you 'do', Pinder; got one of my men killed, not to mention one of yours, too.

No, it didn't.

He tries to move past her, to head back to the communications area, but she cuts him off:

Remember the American drone that went down over Iraq back in 2011?

He doesn't want any part of this conversation, but she's not giving up:

Well do you?

What about it?

Do you know why it went down? I'll tell you why: because the Iraqis, with Chinese help, hacked into its navigation control signal. And from that moment on, everybody, from the National Security Administration to Army Intel, knew that if our remote control frequencies were going to be vulnerable to hacking, then we better have a good back-up plan, so it was back to basics.

'Back to basics'?

'Basics' as in human intel. Otherwise known as spies. And that just happened to be at the same time T Tech was entering its final testing trials.

Kraig considers it cynically:

So that's how you rationalize turning newbies into zombies?

Emily endures his disdain:

As I said, you still don't know what it is I do. Or what T Tech does.

Kraig's had enough:

Me, I'm just following orders. What's your excuse?

He again tries to move past her. But she prevents him:

I'm here to help them, Captain. Anyway I can.

And how's that workin' out for you?

No longer able to endure his disdain, her eyes dig into his:

Like hell, thanks to you.

Kraig smirks:

Right. Because it's all my fault.

He gives her a look and pushes past her to head for his bedroll and a nap. But Emily pursues him:

What if you'd been born here, Captain? What if you'd been raised your whole life to hate the 'foreigners'?

He turns:

Then I'd be one, sad shit, wouldn't I?

To folks here you'd be a hero.

Kraig taps his last reserves of patience:

Just make your point, okay?

She eyes him squarely, sidestepping his mocking tone:

T Tech doesn't change who a person is. It just changes who they think they are. And only for a time, which is what makes Trancers so good at what they do.

Kraig shakes his head, dismissing it all:

Know what I think? I think if you believe that, you're Tranced.

As he moves on, she calls after him:

What I do, what they do, saves lives!

Kraig stops and turns:

You be sure to tell that to Seally's next of kin.

As a soft breeze wells up from the valley below, Masood, his head wounds bandaged, rests on a slope overlooking the two huts and the small goat pen, flanked by Zerak's date tree grove.

Looking down, he notices the self-carved 'U' scrape on his forearm, but he doesn't recognize or remember how it got there, even though there is something familiar about it.

He then looks back out over the slopes to see Tariq, a rifle slung over his shoulder, shepherding goats on a nearby hill, recalling Tariq's accusations, coupled with his own doubts.

Chance – Masood – then wonders to himself:

Am I a spy? If I am, what would be here to spy on? And for whom? The Mezi? Or is it the Americans who are trying to kill me. But why? Why would they want to kill me?

As the questions hang unanswered in his mind, he catches sight of Nadjia going about her chores near the huts. And for just a moment, mesmerized by her graceful movements, captivated by her focused composure, the strife of war seems far away. And as he continues to observe her lonely, breathtaking beauty, he muses in his mind as if speaking to her:

Who are you, Nadjia? Why were you kind to me?

He watches her go back inside the first hut and then lies back and closes his eyes to rest, his mind getting filled with confusing, fleeting visions of…a glistening pond, dancing with the sun's rays as they play across its surface...until:

Mezi!

Masood startles back from his daydream to discover it's already evening, and Tariq is now standing over him, glaring down at the carving on his inner arm.

What is that?

I don't know.

You never know anything, do you? But I know you're a liar and a spy. And I will make you pay for what you are with your life.

He motions for Chance to follow him, so Masood climbs to his feet, still caught in the visions of his dream, and follows Tariq back down to the huts.

An hour later, as Zerak, Nadjia, Tariq, Deqan and Masood eat dinner, seated around a center plate of various foods including cooked rice with dates and okra, all deftly using their fingers to quickly gather food into their mouths, Masood tries to keep pace, eyeing his hosts' skill with envy.

Nadjia notices the look on Masood's face, and it amuses her. But the moment Masood senses her attention and turns his gaze to her, she quickly averts her eyes and moves to clean up.

Later that night, as Masood lies awake, staring into the dark, he hears muffled whispers outside the hut's window.

So he climbs up just enough to peek out of the window to see Tariq gripping Nadjia's arm as Nadjia whispers vehemently:

Let me go!

Bad things happen to whores.

As Nadjia struggles to free herself, she sees Masood spying on her from the hut, peeking from its window, and she tries to gesture to him to hide again, drawing Tariq's attention.

As Tariq turns to see what she was just looking at, Nadjia calls his attention back to her:

You think I am a whore?

Tariq turns back to her:

You touch men you do not know. What do you call that?

I helped someone who needed my help, Tariq.

Tariq sneers imperiously:

One day it will be me you will obey, because you will be mine to do with as I please. So you best please me.

As Tariq's face fills with menace, they hear the goats bleating nearby and Tariq turns to see them wandering about, freed from their pen.

Damn it!

As he hurries to round them back into their pen, Nadjia escapes back into the hut, and catches Masood reentering from the back, fresh from freeing the goats.

They look at each other – Nadjia, aware of what he did – and she offers a small nod, and moves off to her own, curtained area.

By the time Tariq finishes with the goats and steps back into the hut, he finds Masood apparently asleep on the floor and Nadjia back in her quarters, safe from his threats for the moment.

Tariq snorts, frustrated, and heads back to the other hut where he sleeps…

Kraig, stretched out on his bedroll but unable to sleep, finally gives up trying, gets up and moves off to find Riggs at the Satcom station:

Command call yet?

No, but I found this:

He turns the laptop to Kraig displaying a screen filled with Emily's file, replete with an ID photo and biography. Kraig's eyes pop:

How'd you get a hold of this?

This ain't my first rodeo. Anyway, turns out her brother was killed in country. His first tour.

Kraig sobers as Riggs takes back the laptop:

Thought you should know.

As Kraig considers – reconsidering Emily's motivations – the Satcom radio beeps to life and Kraig answers it:

This is Pride Five. Over.

Kraig listens to Command's orders, wincing as he checks his watch:

Copy and roger that, Command. Pride Five out.

Riggs waits as Kraig clicks off to explain:

We got a truck of explosives coming in from Pakistan.

When?

Already on its way.

Within only minutes, the team is on the move again, disguised in Afghan traditional robes, moving through the mountains under a slow-arcing moon.

Minutes lapse into hours as they scale the rough, rocky terrain, heading to intercept their target.

Kraig continually checks his watch along the way, hurrying their pace as Brody and Riggs trade looks, straining to keep up.

Later, they sneak past a Taliban outpost where several fighters with shoulder-mounted anti-aircraft launchers search the night skies for drones, unaware they themselves are being observed.

But tonight these fighters are not the target, so the team moves on undetected, making its way over more peaks and ravines as the dawn breaks over the world to reveal a long, winding mountain road snaking its way along a steep incline through a mountain pass.

Kraig double-checks their GPS coordinates and then turns to his men:

That's gotta be it. Just hope we're not too late.

They hustle down to the road where Riggs quickly moves to deploy a roadside mine:

Well, if it ain't the goddamn cavalry?

They all whip around to see Price and his first lieutenant smirking.

Little on the late-freight, aren't ya, fellas?

Kraig's just about had it with Price.

What are you doing here?

Coverin' for your late, sorry asses.

You're here on orders from Command?

No, I'm here 'cause this Afghan air just does friggin wonders for my complexion.

Kraig knows only too well what happened:

You jumped my orders?

Like I told ya, Kraig: these are my stompin' grounds, so if somethin' needs to get done, I'm your guy.

Just then, they hear the rumble of an approaching truck wending it way up the mountain road.

Somebody needed to be here on time.

As Riggs hurries to position the landmine, Price smirks and holds up the detonation device to his already-positioned mine.

But as long as ya made it, enjoy the show, fellas. Ya just might wanna give us a little elbow room if you know what I mean.

Kraig's eyes burn, but he's forced to motion for his team to take cover.

As they hustle off to hide, Price calls after them:

Don't ya love it when everything just falls into place?

Price and the lieutenant then hustle for cover, taking up positions behind some fallen rocks as the truck in question rumbles around a bend, coming into view.

Kraig, hiding with Brody on the opposite side of the road behind a thicket, uses his rifle's site to check the truck's progress as it whines its way up the narrow road.

It's an old truck, more rust than paint, piled high with grain sacks. As it lumbers along, straining its motor to make the grade, Kraig shakes his head:

Target truck's a blue color. This one's red. Or was red.

As Kraig lowers his rifle and hunkers down to let it pass, they hear a sudden *kaboom* and shock back up to see the old truck suddenly on its side, ablaze, with it load of grain sacks spilling out everywhere like chalk. Kraig is in shock:

What the...!

He then sees Price and his lieutenant emerging from their hiding place to shoot the truck's driver and dazed passenger.

Incensed, Kraig rushes out to confront Price, followed by Brody and Riggs. They run up to the burning truck to find the Afghan farmers dead.

As Price calmly loads another magazine into his semiautomatic, Kraig, livid, surveys the damage. Price sees his consternation and shrugs:

Relax. They like being turned into martyrs.

It was the wrong, goddamn truck, Price! Or doesn't that matter to you?

Price shrugs, glancing over at the burning wreckage and bodies:

Define 'wrong' in a place where everybody and his brother wants to kill you.

As Kraig advances on Price, ready to accost him, they all hear another truck's engine wending its way up the steep road, forcing everybody to rush back to their hiding places as a blue truck lumbers into view, coughing its way up the incline, only to brake and stop at the sight of the still burning truck ahead.

Two armed Afghans climb out of the truck to survey the scene and then call to the driver to turn the truck around.

As the driver gestures that he doesn't have enough room to turn around on this narrow road, the armed men confer and come up with a new plan, motioning the driver to continue slowly as they walk behind him, ready to sacrifice him should this be a trap.

The driver tries to resist, but when they point their guns at him, he obliges, and starts to creep forward…

Kraig, calculating their progress, nods knowingly to Riggs, who stealthily moves off, making his way around the back of the slow-moving truck as it passes by.

Counting off the seconds, Kraig then suddenly springs up and fires on the armed men, who return his fire and quickly hide behind the truck for cover – at which Riggs heaves a grenade at the back of the truck.

But the armed men are able to escape around the truck's side, protecting themselves from the grenade's blast – after which they rally, firing their automatic weapons over the top of the truck at both Kraig and Riggs.

One of their shots wings Kraig's shoulder, dropping him as Price and his lieutenant return fire, killing one of the armed men as the other escapes down the side of the road into a line of trees.

As Price and his lieutenant pursue him, Brody rushes to check on Kraig, pulling back his gear to discover a bleeding wound:

We need to get you some help.

Brody signals to Riggs.

As Riggs hustles back, Price and his lieutenant maneuver into the trees in search of the escaped man, fanning out to try to head him off.

But the man is clearly skilled at evasion, and slips further away, forcing them to continue their hunt in and out of the trees, playing a game of cat-and-mouse, it seems, until they realize they've lost his scent, at which Price spits:

Shit!...Ya see this? This is exactly the kind of fucked up shit that happens when your first goddamn instinct is to befriend these bastards instead of shoot 'em!

He looks around, angry.

Goddamnit!

As the warm afternoon guilds the valley, Masood tries to make himself useful by cleaning out the goat pen.

But Zerak comes over to take the broom from him:

You must rest.

But I want to help.

You are my guest. ...Nadjia?

Nadjia appears in the second hut's doorway:

Something to drink for our guest?

As she moves off to get Masood a drink, Zerak turns back to him:

You're lucky to be alive. Let that be enough for the moment.

Nadjia reappears with a cup of tea and hands it to Masood as Zerak instructs:

See to it that he gets some rest.

Zerak moves off, leaving them alone as Masood drinks the water.

Thank you.

She eyes him, confused, not used to being thanked, and moves off.

He watches after her, captivated, but ever more aware of the danger of this attraction.

As two Taliban fighters, Hakim and Farzad, drink tea, they hear footfalls approaching their cave and reach for their rifles.

A moment later they see the armed man who escaped Price climbing into their cave, breathing hard.

Recognizing him, Hakim and Farzad rush to embrace him:

What happened?

Later that day, as the afternoon quickly chills into evening, Kraig and company arrive back at their cave, exhausted and frustrated. As soon as they arrive Kraig grumbles:

How'd an idiot like Price ever make Captain? Two men dead for no reason; one escaped who will now warn the rest of the Hadj to stay off that road. Goddamnit! It didn't need to go like that!

Brody shrugs:

For something new.

Emily walks up to see Kraig's wound:

You all right?

Fine.

As Kraig tries to get on with his business, Emily persists:

Mind if I take a look? Once upon a time I studied to be a nurse.

He allows her request, but turns back to Brody to continue his rant:

Real question is: why would they give us both the same mission, only not tell us?

Brody shrugs again, used to such snafus.

You need stitches.

Kraig looks over to find Emily offering her diagnosis, which she refines with:

I'd say about thirty stitches.

He dismisses her concern:

Think I'll get a second opinion.

Emily shrugs:

I'll call for an evack.

As she moves to call in a chopper, Kraig scowls:

What? No!

Emily turns back:

Thought you wanted a second opinion?

You're not calling for an evack.

What if it gets infected?

Kraig can't quite believe he's even having this conversation:

What if I get hit by lightning?

She gives him an 'are you kidding me?' wince, but he still insists:

No evack.

He then turns back to Brody:

For every step we take forward, he takes us two steps back.

In the background, Emily begins unpacking a syringe, catching Kraig's notice:

What're you doing?

If you're not taking an evack, then I'm administering a localized antibiotic.

I don't need one.

Yes you do.

No, I don't.

Emily stabs the needle into a vial to extract some of its serum as Kraig looks on, turning pale:

Would you stop it, please?

What's the problem?

I don't want any shots.

You need one.

Kraig gives her a look:

No, I don't. So if you simply need to do something, you can give me a pill, and we'll call it even.

As Kraig turns back to Brody to continue his rant, he hears:
A pill?
Kraig's forced to turn back to her:
Yes, a pill, so it 'doesn't get infected', Nurse.
Emily holds up the syringe, unperturbed:
A shot would be way more effective.
Jesus, no shots! All right? How many times do I need to say it?

She eyes him, suddenly realizing it could be the needle he's afraid of. He sees the look on her face, and becomes even more defensive:
What?
She shakes her head, amazed:
You're kidding, right?
Kidding about what?
She looks at the syringe and then at Kraig:
This is your problem?
Kraig feigns ignorance:
What are you talking about?
You've got how many Hadj out there trying to kill you 24/7, but this is what worries you? A needle?
Kraig's face seems to crinkle, shifting between furious and shaky.
Just give me a goddamn pill, all right?
Emily considers it:
If it helps; first time somebody tried to give me a shot, I fainted.
Kraig looks to Brody:
Would you excuse us?
Sure thing, Cap.
Brody moves off, trying to hide a certain twinkle in his eyes as Kraig turns back to Emily:
No. It doesn't help. Now are we done here?
After I clean your wound, and you take a pill, then we'll be done here.
Kraig's eyes narrow, but he finally accepts her deal.
As she cleans his wounds, they eye each other, discovering a certain sly, subtle sense of humor about it all.
A nurse, huh?

One whole semester's worth.

He looks at her fixedly:

And here I was worried you might know what the hell you were doing!

They trade a look, but soon she refocuses on swabbing his wound.

Masood is awakened by the goats bleating again.

As he gets up, he looks out the window to see Nadjia already doing her chores.

When she sees him, she disappears for a moment, and returns a moment later with a fresh cup of tea. As she hands it to him, he accepts it knowingly:

Thank you.

She smiles, and heads back out to her chores...

Later, Masood is again reclining on the mountainside slope above the orchard as visions of that glistening pond flash up in his memory, but now including a white woman and a black man waving lovingly to him in the way parents do to their children...

He is suddenly startled from his daydream, blinking his eyes to try to halt the effect. He then looks around and sees Nadjia, who is just then looking up from her chores, stealing a glance at him. As their eyes meet, he hears:

How are you feeling?

He turns quickly to find Zerak approaching:

Better. Thank you.

Good.

Zerak surveys the view of his home and orchard from this perch and then kneels beside Masood:

My life. It's not much, but it's more than many have. More than most.

He indicates Tariq:

A hired man.

He then indicates Deqan and Nadjia:

A son. A daughter.

He adjusts himself, getting comfortable:

I had a wife, but she died. Once it was a peaceful life here, and we had more than enough. But now? Now there is only strife. The Americans have come for the Taliban, and when the Taliban want something, they come for us. Not a good arrangement.

Masood nods, appreciating his manner as Zerak inquires:
So tell me about your home.

Masood finds himself wanting to converse with Zerak:
It's like here. But closer to a river, I think.

Zerak seems to understand his struggle:
Don't worry. Your memories will return. And if they don't, you'll make new ones.

As Masood smiles, appreciating his sentiments, Zerak sobers, already on to the real point of this visit:
The important thing is, Nadjia's life is here.

He looks over at Masood:
That is why she must stay here while you, when you are well again, must go. Yes?

Zerak's eyes press into Masood's, compelling a response, so Masood responds in the only way he can:
Yes.

Zerak eases back, satisfied:
Good. I'm glad we had this talk.

Zerak then gets up and moves off.

Masood watches after him and then looks back down to see Nadjia looking up at him from the huts, feeling concern because she knows what her father may have just told him.

That night, as Masood lies awake fingering the scrape marks on his inner arm, he starts hearing the thumping of the chopper's rotors in his mind and sits up, feeling his heart begin to pound out of his chest.

He looks around, suddenly feeling like a stranger in a strange land. But with everyone around him fast asleep, he rides out the panic attack in silence.

As Kraig dozes, he's suddenly startled awake by a Satcom call from Command. Rallying, he climbs to his feet and moves to pick up the receiver:
This is Pride Five, over.

33

Brody and Riggs, nearby, awaken as Kraig listens to Command:

Copy that. Pride Five out.

Kraig clicks off, shaking his head in disbelief as Brody watches him:

What?

Kraig looks over:

They want us to extract him.

Riggs arches a brow:

The dude we just deployed?

Kraig nods as Brody shakes his head, incredulous.

What the fuck?

Kraig offers what details he can:

Seems Command received some Intel about a big attack. They want to know if the Trancer's heard anything. So they need us to extract him long enough for Pinder to do her thing.

Brody looks heavenward:

Would somebody please explain what we ever did to deserve this assignment?

Riggs winks:

You joined Special Forces, dickwad.

Oh right. Almost forgot.

A moment later, Kraig enters Emily's area to find her sleeping akimbo on a cot. He has to chuckle at her position:

Pinder.

As she tries to rally, only partly awake, Kraig continues:

You've got a field debrief in 02 hundreds.

What? You mean...?

We're going mobile.

Emily lunges up to prepare, dropping things in her hurry as Kraig notes her clumsiness, privately amused, and then moves off to Riggs:

See if you can keep her from getting us all killed.

Kraig, Brody, Emily and Riggs move under cover of dark, using their night vision goggles and GPS to make their way back to Zerak's little farm, passing the place where they originally left Chance.

As they near the huts, they stop, and Kraig takes a look through his field binoculars to see Zerak, Deqan, Tariq, Nadjia and Chance, all fast asleep.

Brody looks to Kraig:

What do you think?

Kraig looks on cautiously:

I think we wait this time. See what we're dealing with.

Riggs volunteers:

Copy that.

Kraig then peers back at the huts to see Chance stirring, waking, getting up and wandering out into the night.

What the hell?

Brody looks through their rifle scopes:

What's he doing?

Kraig hands Emily his Night Vision scope, and she takes a look, observing Chance's unsteady movements with a growing concern, which Kraig notes:

What is he doing?

She looks back at Kraig, sobering:

It could be memory flares.

Meaning?

Memory fragments from his real life may be starting to present to his current state of awareness.

Brody shakes his head:

Otherwise known as a meltdown?

Emily shakes her head:

He should never have been deployed in the first place.

Kraig tries to get things back on point:

Just tell me: will it affect our extraction?

Emily considers:

Probably not. But it could effect my debrief. God only knows what's going on in his head at this point. But I won't know until I try.

Brody's eyes roll:

And the hits just keep on comin'!

Emily takes another look through the scope as Brody appeals to Kraig:

We extract him, our job's done here, right?

Emily then decides to tell them more:

There is one other possibility.
They turn to her:
He could be going 'terminal.'
Now Kraig sobers:
'Terminal'?
*If his memory flares increase to the point where they
dislodge his current state of awareness...*
Kraig waits:
Then what?
She looks at Kraig:
Then your 'orders' will be to terminate.
Riggs's ears perk up and he looks over at Emily:
You mean take him out?
Emily nods, at which Brody balks:
*So let me get this straight: you guys screw 'em up so bad
that we have to then take 'em out, is that it?*
Emily, controlled but livid, can't resist:
What's the problem? You did last time.
Brody sobers fast:
Fuck you, lady.
Kraig winces at the prospect. He then looks to Emily:
*You're right. We will take him out, if those are our orders,
but only because once again, what you do will have left us no
other choice.*
Emily's blood boils:
*I told you I didn't want to deploy him in the first place! But
you and Command gave me no choice! So here we all are,
following our fucking orders!*
She glares at all of them – which they have to accept,
however begrudgingly, because they know she's right.
Kraig then takes another look at Chance to see him still
wandering in the dark of night...

Chance, lost in his dream, is wading into that glistening
pond, looking back to see that white woman and a black man
waving to him...
The scene then shifts, and he finds himself riding in the
back of a truck, looking up from the back seat as the white
woman drives, humming to herself cheerfully...

Brody draws in a deep breath, steeling himself:
So, Cap? What do you want to do?
Kraig checks his watch:
It'll be light in 40 minutes. I say we wait.
He looks to Emily, inviting her opinion:
Probably not a good time to try to debrief him, anyway.
Kraig welcomes her decision:
Okay, let's see if we can get a little closer, wait out the day and, all things being equal, extract him tomorrow night.

The sun's rays find Chance – Masood – dozing on the ground, until a gun-barrel jabs into his cheek.
Masood wakes up with a start to find Tariq glowering down at him:
Spy! I knew it!

A minute later, Tariq shoves Masood in front of Zerak, who asks him:
Where did you go last night?
Nowhere!
Zerak's brow furrows:
Then why did you go outside?
I...don't know.
Tariq grumbles:
Liar.
Zerak looks to Tariq:
Where'd you find him?
Near the goats.
Are any of the goats missing?
Tariq sniffs:
No. But he is a Mezi, and the Mezi steal sheep!
Zerak looks back at Tariq:
And how do you know that, having never gone anywhere near the Mezi?
Tariq tenses:
Because I hear things!
Zerak turns calmly back to Masood:
I don't think even the Mezi spy on goats.

Tariq, momentarily stymied, then spots the partial 'U' scraping on the inside of Masood's forearm.

And what is that?

Tariq points. Zerak inspects Masood's arm and then looks to Masood for an answer:

How did you get this?

Masood shakes his head, at a loss as Tariq accuses:

It's his identification!

Zerak ponders it:

Or merely a scratch.

He is a spy. I know it!

Or a sleep-walker, Tariq. Either way, that will be all, thank you.

Tariq, frustrated, shoulders his rifle and withdraws as Zerak looks back at Masood:

A man who sleep-walks is searching for something. So what is it that you are searching for, Masood?

Later that morning, Masood is again sitting by himself, looking down at the two huts and worrying, Zerak's simple question still echoing inside...

Not far away, hidden behind a row of wild bushes, Kraig, Emily, Brody and Riggs await their turn. As Riggs keeps watch, Emily, dozing, rolls over to find herself face to face with Kraig, who opens his eyes to feel an unexpected surge of attraction.

She then opens her eyes, too, realizing how close they are, and pulls back, trying to restore order:

So you'll extract him tonight?

Kraig turns to check with Riggs, wincing as he rolls over onto his wounded shoulder.

Riggs signals a 'thumbs up', so Kraig rolls back to face Emily, suppressing a wince at his still wounded shoulder:

Yes.

Emily, sensing they've both recoiled into coolness, so she tries to ease things, whispering:

How's your shoulder?

Fine. Check your equipment. I don't want to extract him for nothing.

Emily maneuvers to run some quick system checks on her laptop, using a spray bottle cleaner to wipe the Afghan dust off its screen.

Looking over her shoulder, Kraig sees a high-speed video image of an Afghan woman talking in Pashtu:

What's that?

Part of his implanted memory sequences. This is his mother.

Kraig looks on confused:

His 'mother'?

Like any of us, a Trancer needs these kinds of memories to confirm who he thinks he is.

Kraig eyes it, with a feeling somewhere between incredulous and horrified, as Emily eyes his reaction:

We all need our stories. And we all have them.

Kraig doesn't like the sound of that:

The only difference is the rest of us have real memories. Not made-up stories.

Emily smiles:

Really? How about the story of who you are, or why you're here, or why you do what you do?

Kraig balks:

Those are reasons. Not stories.

She parries:

They're stories that give you your reasons.

He shakes his head, not wanting to be drawn in, but unable to resist:

You make it sound like we just make our lives up as we go.

In most ways we do, based on what happens to us in life and how we deal with it.

Think you're confusing 'story' with facts.

She's heard this line of argument before:

Am I? Then define what you mean by a 'fact'?

Kraig shakes his head, realizing he's now committed himself to this argument.

The fact of who we are. Which is not just some random idea or made-up 'story' we come up with to explain ourselves to ourselves.

She smiles knowingly:

I never said our stories were random.

Brody and Riggs, who have been monitoring this conversation, shake their heads dismissively, which Emily notes:

Don't believe me?

Kraig shrugs:

Looks like the consensus is 'no'; we don't believe you.

Emily considers how to explain:

Okay, say you're in some bar—

Brody rallies:

A bar? I'm in!

And a woman comes up to you—

Riggs interrupts:

A brunette?

Emily shrugs:

Sure. A brunette.

But Riggs looks disappointed:

Really? Cause I'm really more of a red-head guy.

Brody's jaw drops:

A Red-head?! Never pegged you for a red-head dude.

Riggs argues back:

With a name like Brody, shouldn't you be like all over red-heads?

Emily tries to continue her point:

Anyway, if this woman – this red-head – asks you what your story is . . .

But Riggs and Brody are still negotiating hair color, with Brody asserting:

Sorry, bro, but I'll take a brunette any day over a red-head.

Emily tries once more:

Whatever her hair color, fellas, what do you tell her?

Riggs finally looks back at Emily:

Would this be before or after I tell her I'm from the planet Krypton?

Kraig has to chuckle as Emily digs in:

No, Riggs. I meant after she tells you you're full of shit.

Brody grins:

Hooya.

Emily turns to Brody, challenging him, too:

So what do you tell her, Brody?

Guess I tell her where I'm from.

He shoots a sly look towards Riggs and Kraig:

And that I like babies and puppies, and that I cry a lot at chic flicks.

Kraig and Brody have to suppress an urge to guffaw as Emily shakes her head, ready to drop it. But as they continue to be amused at her expense, she reconsiders and rises to their challenge:

My point is: you tell her the same story you've been telling yourself so many times that you actually think it's true.

Kraig takes issue:

But if I'm from Des Moines, and I tell her I'm from Des Moines, how's that not a fact?

Emily looks to Kraig:

Because those 'facts' are not what's important. It's the story you, me, any of us, make of the facts. So even if all of us were from Des Moines, all with very similar backgrounds, it still come down to the story we create around those similar backgrounds that define us, first and foremost to ourselves. And if you think people can be extreme about their religious beliefs, try telling them their story's just a story, and not a fact.

She gives them a look, indicating their over-reactions to her comments have already proven her point.

But Kraig isn't persuaded:

So we're all just walking around in some dream-story of our own making, is that it?

Pretty much.

Riggs suddenly hand-signals for silence.

Kraig and Brody instantly maneuver to see what Riggs sees: Tariq and the two Afghan fighters, armed, are talking as they shepherd the goats right towards them.

Kraig whips back around to warn Emily as Riggs and Brody ready the M1's for battle.

As the Afghans guide the goats closer and closer to their hideout, Kraig, Brody and Riggs train their guns on them, fingering their triggers. The goats, meanwhile, approach their leafy cover and, despite seeing the team hiding in its leaves, begin to nibble away at the thin layers of foliage that are keeping them hidden.

Brody and Riggs now look to Kraig for instructions: Do we fire now, or wait?

As Kraig considers, Zerak joins the fighters, also carrying a rifle, and strikes up a conversation with Tariq. Meanwhile, the goats continue to munch away at the leaves, slowly but surely exposing Kraig and company to view.

Kraig's mind races and he suddenly feels Emily trying to hand him something.

He turns to her to see she's urging her cleaning fluid on him, indicating he should spray it at the goats.

Kraig takes the bottle and, as quietly as he can, reaches it out to spray it at the goats, which instantly recoil as the spray mists their noses.

Offended by its scent, they bleat and abruptly move off to graze elsewhere.

Tariq, Zerak and Deqan, none the wiser, follow their goats onwards, bypassing Kraig and company.

Back near the huts, Nadjia, going about her daily chores, sees Masood walking in the orchard, looking pensive.

Checking if the coast's clear, she abandons what she's doing to secretly move to him, surprising him when he looks up to find her standing nearby.

In any other world, they would run to each other, take hold of this moment and begin a life of their own.

But standing in this orchard, stealing this brief moment together, the most they can do is hold each others' gaze, wary of immense danger of being discovered.

But Nadjia, increasingly finding her courage, moves to Masood to say:

You look sad.

He eyes her for some time before replying:

So do you.

She nods, but a small, fleeting smile finds her lips as she acknowledges this most fundamental condition of her life:

Are you, sad?

He smiles and says:

I don't know what I am.

She kneels, signaling an ever-deepening comfort with him, and kneels beside him as she shrugs:

Life.

She looks over. Their eyes meet, finding a solace in each other, which encourages her to ask:

Do you ever wonder what life is like somewhere else?

He smiles knowingly as she continues:

Why do I wonder such things?

He smiles:

Because you want to leave here. To see if life can be different. Because you have hope that it can.

She shakes her head:

'Hope'? Yes, but...no.

Not even in your dreams?

She looks down:

Hopeful dreams are the cruelest of all.

Nadjia?

She tenses at the sound of Tariq's gruff voice, calling her from a distance.

She gives Masood a fleeting, yearning look before hurrying off, filled with a hope that scares her.

Later, they all gather for dinner again, but Masood pretends to take no notice of her.

As night fills the sky, opening to the cosmos above, Kraig checks out the layout of the two huts via his scope:

Assuming he'll be in the second structure on the left, we'll approach from the North, and—

Brody suddenly interjects:

We got company, 11 o'clock!

Brody points and Kraig pans his scope to see Hakim and Farzad, the two Taliban fighters, arriving from the south.

What the hell do they want?

Hakim and Farzad arrive and Deqan hides as the others step out to meet them.

The fighters demand food and water, so Zerak directs Nadjia to bring them what they want.

Kraig watches them, irked:
Like they own the place.

Hakim then points at Tariq, summarily conscripting him into the Taliban.

Brody's none too concerned:
Looks like somebody just got his ass drafted.

As Tariq, shocked by his sudden troubles, turns pale, Brody chuckles:
That's right, you love the Taliban, don't ya boy!

Nadjia's pulse quickens – could this be the miraculous answer to her prayers?

She watches as Tariq obligingly moves to join their ranks, knowing that he has no choice, and she can barely contain her joy.

But then she begins to worry again as Tariq, putting on a show of elaborate humility, moves to Farzad to whisper something in his ear.

Farzad listens, apparently receptive.

Kraig, watching via his scope, wonders:
What's he up to?
Riggs shrugs:
He's up to something all right.

A moment later, Farzad moves to Hakim to confer.

Nadjia looks on, her stomach in knots, as Hakim suddenly points at Masood, and releases Tariq:

Kraig blanches:
What the hell? Did they just make a switch?

Masood meanwhile sobers and hesitates, until Farzad points his rifle at him, forcing his compliance.

Masood then looks to Zerak for help, but Zerak can't help him.

He then looks to Nadjia, who returns his look, her eyes burning, devastated, as Hakim commands:
Let's go!

And they start off, heading back into the mountains with Masood, their new conscript, in tow.

Tariq, flushing with a sneer, watches after them and then turns to share his delight with Nadjia, who nearly falls to her knees.

Riggs looks on, frustrated, checking his GPS:
They're definitely heading back into tribal territory.
Kraig scowls:
Goddamnit.
Emily looks around:
So what do we do?
Kraig considers their options:
Only goddamn thing we can do.
At which the team gathers up its equipment to track Masood, now a newly-minted Taliban fighter, regardless of who and what his life may have been before...

As the long night rolls past midnight, Farzad notes Masood's scarf:
Mezi?
Masood nods.
Be happy, Mezi. This way you will die like a man. Not a sheepherder.

Keeping pace behind Masood at a stealthy distance, Brody looks over at Emily, reminded once more of why her work disgusts him:
The folks at T Tech ever actually think any of this shit through? Like how your Vulcan mind-meld bull-crap might actually play out in the real world?
Kraig shoots Brody a look:
Enough.
And they trudge on, tracking Masood and his Taliban escorts.

As Hakim and Farzad lead Masood further north, Kraig and company continue to keep track until they see them all stopping on a plateau.

Brody checks through his gun site:
What are they up to?
Kraig's watching though his site:
Looks like they're bedding down.
As Hakim and Farzad start to clear a space to sleep, tossing aside rocks, Masood eyes the area warily, which Farzad questions:
Why are you looking around like that?
We shouldn't sleep here.
Hakim looks over:
Why not?
Masood shrugs as if it's obvious:
Because the Americans can see us here.
He indicates the sky above them.
Hakim reconsiders, looks around, and spots an area in a ravine below.
Then down there.
And they make their way from the plateau into a ravine.

As Kraig and Brody watch Hakim and Farzad seek out cover after Masood's warning, it gives Kraig an idea:
See that? See what just happened?
Brody nods, but Emily and Riggs are lost.
Your guy just warned 'em off that mesa.
Kraig looks back to Brody:
You thinking what I'm thinking?
Brody nods, grinning:
It would definitely give him some instant street cred.
Now Riggs gets what they mean, but Emily's still at a loss:
What would give him street cred?
But Kraig's already turning back to Brody:
There a bird in range?
As Brody contacts command via the Satcom, Kraig hands his scope to Emily. She takes it and looks through it as he directs her:
See that mesa? Keep your eyes on it.
Why? What are you going to do?
As Emily looks through the scope, Brody motions a thumbs-up to Kraig:

On my spot.

As Brody waits for acknowledgment from Command, Kraig takes out his soflam laser and targets at the mesa:

Okay, bring it.

As Farzad lights a small campfire, settling in, he engages Masood more like a friend now than a conscript:

So, how were you injured?

Drone attack.

Ah. So that is why you are afraid of open places.

Just then, they hear a high-pitched whistle followed by a thundering blast, and they look up from the ravine to see an explosion boil into a fireball at the exact spot they just vacated.

Farzad gapes in shock and then turns slowly back to Masood.

How did you know?

Hakim, equally impressed, looks to Masood:

Yes, how did you?

Masood calmly shrugs, even if he can't quite remember why:

Experience.

Farzad and Hakim exchange a stunned look of relief.

...Allahu akbar, Masood.

Emily puts down the scope to eye Kraig and Brody, as Kraig grins:

Now when he says something, they'll listen.

Brody chimes in:

Instant street cred.

Emily starts to appreciate the method to their madness.

Not far away, Price and his lieutenant are looking on through their scopes, alerted by the Hellfire missile strike:

What the hell was that for?

He glances at his lieutenant, thinking out loud:

Do-Right's definitely up to some bullshit. And we're gonna find out what.

As Hakim, Farzad and Masood settle in for the night, enjoying the safety of the ravine, Hakim offers:

I will take the first shift, Farzad the second, and you the last.

As Hakim moves off, Farzad looks to Masood:

See that? Already he trusts you. Which is why you should know the reason we need fighters is because something is coming. Something big. And it will involve all of us.

Involve us how?

An attack. In Jalalabad. Next month. Our biggest ever, after which we will all meet again in Paradise!

Farzad is excited, clearly expecting a day of glory as Masood rolls over to rest, getting filled with foreboding.

Later that night, as Masood keeps watch, manning his shift perched on a rock, he suddenly doubles over as if punched hard in the gut.

As he gropes for air, incapacitated, Kraig and Brody emerge from the shadows to jab a tranquilizer into him, further incapacitating him before carting him quickly away.

They arrive back to lay Masood – Chance – by Emily's equipment. She pastes diodes to his temples and then clicks a code into her laptop. Chance's body braces up and then collapses, unconscious.

As she checks his pulse, he slowly revives, looking up at her lost and confused, reeling back into himself as if back, awakening from a coma:

Wha...What's –

Emily leans in close:

It's okay. Relax. You're safe now. Do you know who I am?

She rises up so that he can see her face. He eyes her, vaguely recognizing her. But before he can piece together who she is, she's already asking:

We need to know if you've heard anything about a coming attack.

Chance doesn't seem to understand, so she tries to clarify:

On us.

He still looks lost.

48

On U.S. Forces?

It takes him a moment, but it all finally starts coming back to him:

...An attack. In Jalalabad.

When?

Next month. Their biggest ever.

Their biggest attack ever on what?

Chance's face suddenly sobers as if he just realized he might be betraying a secret. As he clams up, Emily presses for answers:

Attack on what, Chance?

She eyes him, noting his conflicted look of desperation, sensing he may be shifting:

You are an American Soldier. You understand me? Your name is Gavin Chance. You grew up in Macon, Georgia. You have a sister.

But his pulse starts to spike. She glances up to find Kraig, out of Chance's sight-line, looking on intently, wondering what's going on.

Emily can't explain at the moment, so she refocuses on Chance as he starts to come back into himself, shifting back into his American identity:

Just try and relax, Chance, okay?

We've got to stop it!

Stop the attack?

Yes!

And we will, thanks to you.

He looks at her, suddenly becoming confused again:

Me? How can I stop it?

We need to know exactly when and on what the attack in Jalalabad will be. Understand?

His eyes burn.

But how am I supposed to find that out?

Emily eyes him, realizing he doesn't recall he's a Trancer, and she looks to Kraig, who moves into Chance's view to say:

Because we're sending you back in.

Back into what?

Your mission.

Chance turns to Emily, terrified. But she doesn't know how to console him as he starts to become aware of the diodes and the laptop, vaguely reminding him that he volunteered for this – even if he can't remember for what.

My mission. But I don't wanna die.

Emily falters. She looks up, appealing to Kraig's better angels, and sees a look in his eyes she's never seen before, as if he's suddenly seeing Chance as a soldier and brother:

Corporal, you can save lives if you go back in. Do you understand?

Chance sobers:

Then I...better go back.

He looks to Emily, assuring her that's what he wants, and reluctantly, deeply conflicted, she moves to click the necessary key on her laptop.

She then looks up at Kraig, silently committing him to decision. She then presses the key, sending a consciousness-crashing jolt through Chance's fragile body.

Kraig and Brody reposition Chance – Masood – back where they found him, perched at his look-out post, and then retreat into the night.

They rejoin Emily and Riggs, and continue on, withdrawing to higher ground.

As they move off, Brody looks to Kraig:

Where to, Cap?

East, towards those trees.

Kraig then moves to consult Emily:

Is he going to be okay?

She doesn't respond. Kraig looks over. She is brimming with emotions; all she can do is to shrug that she doesn't know.

Kraig tries to reassure her:

We're going to stay close. Anything happens, and we extract him for good.

Emily considers it and then looks back at Kraig:

Thought you were the guy who'd deploy him no matter what?

Those are my orders.

But you're ready to extract him without any orders?

Kraig doesn't have a good explanation for that:
Let's just say I might have to make a field decision.
They trade a knowing look.
Kraig's gaze sharpens as they come to a new set of terms:
What are you doing here, Pinder?
You first.
He gives her a look, considering how much he's willing to say:

Me, I always wanted to be a soldier. A good soldier....Guess I thought I could do some good.
Surprised and affected by his sudden openness, Emily looks over:
Me, too.
He looks over, sensing an undercurrent in her answer:
But not anymore?
Are you asking me that? Or are you asking yourself that?
He considers how to answer, recoiling back into his shell, and counters with:
So T Tech's your baby, huh?
Something like that.
A few beats pass as they continue. But something's boiling up in Kraig, and he suddenly turns to confront her:
Thing about following orders? Sometimes they're just the easy way out.
Out of what?
Out of having to explain to yourself what you're doing, as opposed to the good you thought you'd be doing....Kind of like those stories you say we tell ourselves.
They eye each other, coming to terms as Brody and Riggs, leading the way, pause, waiting for them to catch up. But Emily is in no hurry as she looks into Kraig's eyes, finally getting a sense of who he really is, until...A laser signal flashes in their wake.
Kraig instinctively drives Emily to the ground, covering her as Riggs and Brody poise for battle, only to hear a familiar chuckle approaching their position.
Kraig grimaces as Brody and Riggs exchange a disgusted look, recognizing Price's unmistakable voice:
Pussies, all.

Price and his lieutenant stroll into view, grinning, but do a double-take when they see Emily:

Whoa! Not exactly where I'd take a date, bro, but hey, you're the man, right?

As Kraig and Emily climb back to their feet:

What do you want, Price?

For starters? Some goddamn answers.

Kraig stonewalls him:

Like I said: you follow your orders, I'll follow mine. But so help me, you do that shit again, and we will engage.

Price balks:

Ooh, scary. But you still haven't told me who the smokin' hot is?

Emily's about to answer, but Kraig gestures this is his to handle:

If Command didn't tell you, Price, that's your problem. Not ours.

Kraig turns to his team:

Let's move.

As they head on their way, Price calls to them:

I am gonna find out what's goin' on Kraig. You know I will.

Kraig ignores him. Keeps moving. Out of Price's earshot, Emily whispers to Kraig:

Who the hell was that?

Just a little slice of Heaven.

He's got a big mouth.

And a big gun. Just not a big brain.

They hike in the darkness over mountain terrain under a sliver of a moon. As they do, Emily eyes Kraig, still recalling their earlier conversation.

A moment later, Brody hears a communiqué in his hear, and rushes forward to consult Kraig:

We got Hadj headed our way, 1 tick north.

Kraig grimaces:

How'd they find us?

Riggs steps up:

It's gotta be our signal.

They're tracking our signal?

They hacked that drone, didn't they? And it would explain how they managed to ambush us before.

Emily shoots Brody a knowing look, reminding him that he had earlier accused her Trancer of ratting them out.

Brody tries to ignore it, but Kraig notes Emily's tacit point and takes the possibility to heart:

Which means, maybe she was right. But either way, we're in a new ball game.

Kraig takes up the Satcom and calls Command:

This is Pride Five. Over. Pride Five. Do you read?

Roger that, Pride Five. We read you loud and clear. Over.

Requesting 'Fortify', over.

Roger Fortify, Pride Five. Over.

Pride Five, out.

Emily waits for an explanation, but then is finally forced to ask:

What's all that about?

Riggs offers:

Special Ops Pig Latin for we think our signal's being hacked.

Emily considers its implications:

As in 'allway uckedfay upway'?

Riggs shakes his head:

I never understood pig-Latin. But somehow I understood that.

So how we avoid the Hadj?

Kraig checks his GPS:

We go north by north east, then cut back to keep track of Chance.

He then throws a look to Brody and Riggs, who seem to instinctively know what he means, even if Emily doesn't.

As they hike along, Emily hears a distance buzzing sound which soon grows into the rumble of chopper approaching.

She looks over to Kraig, quickly deducing what this means:

What's goin' on?

An extraction.

Kraig laser guides the chopper down and then hurries the team over to it.

As Brody and Riggs replenish and resupply for their packs with food, water and ammo, Kraig turns to Emily:

Time for you to go.

She grimaces, her suspicions confirmed.

No way.

Kraig insists:

They'll be coming after us heavy now.

So?

So we'll take it from here, Pinder.

She shakes her head, resolute:

I have a man in the field. I'm not leaving, Captain.

Which is why we're going back to extract him, Pinder.

Emily balks:

But what if something goes wrong?

Kraig's getting frustrated:

Goddamnit, Emily, we're trained for this.

And I'm trained for Trancers, which you're not, Jeff!

He notes her use of his first name as the Chopper pilot shouts:

Is she coming or not?

Emily shouts back:

No!

The pilot, confused, looks to Kraig – at which he eyes Emily intensely, quickly realizing she isn't going anywhere.

So he pounds on the chopper's hull, signaling the pilot, and the Chopper lifts away, disappearing into the night.

Kraig watches it go and then shoots Emily a quick, frustrated look after which he signals to Brody and Kraig, and they all move out into the darkness.

As Hakim and Farzad build a fire, Masood, looking as if he's lost in a dream, observes them, thinking to himself:

They seem to know me. To trust me. I must be one of them.

But as the fire flickers to life, it triggers his memory flashbacks, and he soon finds himself riding in that car again with that white woman at the wheel, humming cheerfully to herself, when the truck is suddenly struck violently by a speeding car.

And a moment later, he's opening his eyes to see the car he was just in is flipped over on its side, burning up as the woman calls for help.

As he struggles up to try to help her, he hears:

Masood?...Masood?

He is shocked awake, opening his eyes to see Farzad and Hakim looking down at him, alarmed:

Are you all right?

He can't find his words, so Hakim looks to Farzad, worried:

Maybe he needs to eat something.

As Masood looks around, realizing he must have fainted, Hakim takes out a pomegranate and offers it.

Masood eyes it, suddenly reminded of Nadjia. Farzad senses his preoccupation:

What?

It reminds me of someone.

Farzad smiles, cuts it open and tears off a wedge for him:

Pomegranates remind me of my mother. And it is for her that I fight.

For your mother?

Farzad shrugs. Smiles.

For Masood, the memory reminds him of the car accident, of the woman's cries for help...

Masood?

Masood starts back to the present:

Are you sure you all right?

Yes.

As Masood sucks on some pomegranate seeds, Farzad reflects:

Truth is, I also fight for myself. For the world I know.

Farzad looks around, suddenly turning sober:

All these inventions of the West only they understand, how will I survive in such a world? What will Farzad do? What will become of my village? My tribe? How will I feed my family? You can't eat a computator.

You mean a computer?

Humiliated, Farzad admits:

Yes.

Masood then asks:

I need a favor. Will you help me?
Help you what?

Kraig, leading his team forward, pauses to assess the terrain and then says:
Long as they're stopped, we'll rest here.

A little later, hidden in the trees, Kraig, Emily, Brody and Riggs are lying close together, munching on MRE energy bars and listening to Riggs whisper a story to bide their time:
So this 5-jump-chump's talkin' like he's Rambo. So I ask where he trained, and guess what he says: Fort Lee.
Brody shakes his head:
Fort Leisure?
Dude was serious!
They all chuckle, except Emily, who's utterly lost, and Kraig takes pity:
Fort Lee trains mostly cooks. Not Rambos.
But Brody can't leave it there and so grins:
Bunch of cherry-ass FNG fuzz bars.
Emily looks to Kraig for another translation:
FNG: Fuckin' New Guy. 'Fuzz' 'cause of their velcro patches.
Brody then looks to Riggs, teasing him:
So ya tell him where you trained?
Bet your ass, I did.
Emily, trying to get into this back and forth, asks:
Where?
Riggs takes up her challenge:
Fort Wood.
At which Kraig can't resist adding:
Try Fort fuckin' lost-in-the-woods.
Riggs chuckles knowingly, conceding:
Thought I'd never get outta that damn forest. How bout you, Cap?
Me? I was fried and dried at Fort Bliss.
Riggs shakes his head:
Fuckin' Fort Blister?
Kraig nods while Brody shakes his head:

I'd take Fort Lost-in-the-Woods over Blister any day.

Kraig sees Emily trying to understand, so he adds:

Try the middle of Texas, and hot like a sonofabitch. Dropped 20 pounds just getting through basic.

So where'd you guys meet?

Riggs volunteers:

Fort Campbell. But we trained at Fort Bragg.

Brody scoffs:

Better known as 'Fort Drag'.

Emily looks again to Kraig for an explanation:

Not a lot of women folk at Fort Drag.

As Emily grins, Brody eyes at her, ready to finally make up his mind about her one way or another:

So what's your story? What made you wanna come down range with some snake-eaters like us?

Kraig waits, interested to hear what she'll say.

She notes Kraig's interest and then turns to Brody:

My brother.

What about him?

He was part of the 25th, training Afghan Police, when one of them shot and killed him.

They all sober, waiting to hear more, so she continues:

I was working in New Mexico at the time. The day I got the call, I was sitting in this nice, clean, air-conditioned office. And when his commanding officer told me what happened I thought: how can I be sitting in here, all safe and sound, and he dies lying in the dirt of some street halfway around the world, with no one there to even say good-bye to.

Her eyes well up:

After that, I...I kinda had to come.

As they eye each other, coming to a new understanding, Riggs suddenly shunts up a hand, signaling for silence:

Kraig and Brody instantly get ready for action, hearing unseen footfalls crunching the dirt nearby. They hold their collective breath as more footfalls crunch the ground, closing in on their position.

Kraig fingers his trigger, glancing to Riggs who's peering intensely via a night scope, using hand signals to indicate there are five fighters approaching them.

Kraig looks knowingly to Brody, who quietly un-clips a hand grenade from his vest as Kraig indicates to Emily that when Brody throws the grenade, they'll all make a run for it.

He looks back to Brody, who maneuvers carefully to free his throwing hand cradling the grenade.

Riggs indicates the direction and distance Brody should throw, and Kraig then silently counts him down...

Brody heaves the grenade. Seconds later, a fighter suddenly cries out in the dark, followed by an ear-busting *kaboom* – at which Kraig, Emily, Riggs and Brody all jump to their feet, firing as they make their running retreat...

Taliban fighters fire back from the shadows, their muzzles flashing with a steady barrage of bullets as Kraig and company maneuver into a ravine.

Kraig, keeping Emily behind him, guides them behind a row of rocks and then signals Brody to cover him as he moves back out into the night.

Riggs and Brody keep up a fierce round of counter-fire as Kraig sneaks around to the Taliban's flank, moving like a shadow in the pitch blackness.

As he edges forward, nearing his target, working his way into what looks like a clear line of fire from behind a tree, sensing immanent victory, he is suddenly confronted by a Taliban fighter, equally stunned, stepping out from behind the same tree.

The fighter instinctively lunges at Kraig and they tumble to the ground in a combat to the death as Kraig, barely avoiding the fighter's knife swipe at his head, deftly deflects its force while using his free hand to draw his service pistol and shoot the man in the gut.

Kraig quickly retrieves his M4 again and repositions himself to aim and fire, spraying a storm of bullets into the Taliban's position.

One rears up, struck, firing wildly before collapsing.

Riggs, still firing on the Taliban from behind the row of rocks, suddenly pitches backwards, struck by one of a dying fighter's errant shots.

Emily scrambles over to Riggs, now on his back and bleeding from a chest wound as Brody shouts:

How is he?
We've got to stop the bleeding!

Back on the Taliban's flank, Kraig takes out two more fighters and then hurries back as Emily, by Riggs's side, peels back his gear to put pressure on the bleeding wound. A moment later, Kraig hustles back into view just as Brody wields around, about to shoot him. But he checks himself just in time as Kraig grabs the sitcom and calls Command:

Mayday, Mayday, Mayday, this is Pride Five. I need a Medevac now! Do you copy?

Emily applies pressure on Riggs's wound:
Hang in there!

Brody fires more rounds into the dark just to make sure as Kraig leans in close to reassure Riggs:
They're coming for you, bro, so just hang in there.
Then to Brody:
We got to get him to a spot!

Minutes later, they carry Riggs to an open area where Kraig takes out his soflam to target a landing position for the chopper's pilot.

Riggs meanwhile looks up at Emily, breaking into a grin:
And here I was worried about you.
We're gonna get you out of here.
As he chokes up blood, the chopper touches down.

Kraig, Emily and Brody rush Riggs to its bay, and load him in. Kraig then looks at Emily and shouts:
Go with him.
No!

Kraig, incredulous, pounds once more on the chopper's hull, and it lifts away into the night.

As Kraig, Emily and Brody rush back into the dark, Kraig is already back on a call to Command:
This is pride five requesting a track on any Hadj movements at coordinates November Tree-five-six-point-two, Echo seven-zero-tree. Do you copy, over?
Wilco, Pride Five. Stand by, tracking as we speak. Over.

In a dark cubicle, a drone Pilot sits at what looks like a game station, piloting what appears to be a video game layout over Afghanistan airspace. Only it's a real drone, and in real time.

On his monitor, the drone Pilot watches black and white images beamed back from the drone's nose camera as it pans the terrain to see a small band of fighters moving with their wounded, heading for Zerak's two huts.

On the ground, Zerak, Nadjia and Deqan, unaware, are asleep when the fighters arrive to rouse them from their rest. Hearing their calls for help, Zerak rises warily to meet them.

He steps out to see two Taliban men carrying a third, badly injured fighter.

They exchange some quick words in Pashtu, after which Zerak directs them into the second hut.

As they enter, Tariq rises to make room for the injured man:

Nadjia, water!

As Zerak dutifully confers with the fighters, Nadjia enters with water.

Tariq gives her a menacing look, implicitly warning her not to touch this wounded man.

As Nadjia pushes past Tariq to assist in the fighter's triage, Zerak sees the byplay between Nadjia and Tariq and, using it as an excuse to keep Nadjia away from the fighters, makes a show of yelling at them:

Both of you, leave now!

Nadjia leaves and Tariq follows, passing Deqan on his way into the second hut.

Nadjia, momentarily banished from the second hut, steps back into the first hut, followed by Tariq.

Locked on target and standing by. Over.
Roger that, Over.

As Kraig, Emily and Brody crest a hill, they see Zerak's two huts on the adjoining mountainside:

What do you want to do?
We'll wait here. They'll be on the move again soon enough.

As they catch their breath slowly, a hellfire missile suddenly streaks down from the sky to explode into the second hut, instantly leveling it into a pile of burning rubble.

Kraig is shocked as the target bursts up in flames:

No! Goddamnit!

As Emily, Brody and Riggs look on stunned at the destruction, Kraig grabs the Satcom radio:

Pride Five to base, Pride five to base. Do you read me, over?

We read you, Pride Five, over.

What the fuck was that, goddamnit?

Stand by, Pride Five.

Back at the remaining hut, Nadjia, dazed, staggers out to see the pile of burning rubble that was the second hut.

Horrified, she starts frantically combating the smoke and flames to search for Zerak and Deqan, screaming for Tariq's help.

But Tariq, worried there might be yet another strike, hurries away as Nadjia screams after him:

Coward!

She then screams to the skies:

Cowards!!

Kraig, livid, is still waiting for Command's explanation:

Pride Five, over.

Roger, Pride Five. Stand by over.

Kraig's pacing, all but jumping out of his skin:

I requested tracking, not targeting, over!

Roger that, Pride Five. Targeting granted to Spotter Unit operating in your sector.

What fucking spotter unit?

Then it dawns:

Price!

Kraig peers again through his scope to see Nadjia sobbing on her knees by the burning rubble pile, which has now become the grave of her father and little brother.

Kraig's face fills with the revulsion of a man who has come to the end of his tether. Emily steps to him, shaken:

Why? Why'd he do it?

For the same reason that the Afghan shot your brother. For the same reason this will go on and on and on. Long as there's an 'us' and a 'them', it'll never stop.

Hakim, Farzad, and Chance are all listening to a Tribal Elder describing the attack they will be a part of:

Twelve simultaneous attacks across Pakistan, designed to inflict the greatest possible damage.

A Bomb-Maker holds up a rusty nail.

The explosives will be packed with these, to assure the greatest possible number of injuries. Then, as help arrives, the second explosives will detonate, ensuring even greater casualties.

As the men nod approvingly amongst themselves, they hear:

Why?

All eyes turn to Masood:

Why kill and injure the innocent?

The Elder takes exception:

Because those who would help our enemies are our enemies!

Masood considers it and then asks:

But what if they are simply men and women trying to help their fallen brothers and sisters? Does not Allah bless the merciful?

The Elder sniffs, certain of his convictions:

The innocent will go to Paradise.

Yes, but why is it for you to decide when they go?

The Elder's eyes darken with umbrage:

We are the victims. We are the attacked. And while we may not have missiles that fall from the sky, we can still control what happens here on the ground! That is why we shall take an eye for an eye.

And when we are all blind, and they are all blind, what then?

Those around Masood glare at him, prompting Farzad to roughly 'escort' Masood out of the meeting, making a show to satisfy the others that he's as offended as they are by Masood's insolent questions.

Once outside and out of earshot, Farzad confronts Masood:

*What were you thinking in there? Why could you not hold
your tongue?*

Masood eyes Farzad coolly:

How could you hold yours?

*Because I value it! Look: you saved my life. For that, I will
always be grateful. But not if you now get me killed!*

Hakim runs up, looking serious:

*Get him away from here, and only because you saved our
lives. But after this, we are even!*

As Hakim moves off again, Farzad turns to Masood:

*You think we are not men of honor? Well I will prove to
you we are by honoring my promise. After that, you will honor
our struggle, and come with me to Jalalabad, where you and I
will martyr ourselves for the Creator. Agreed? Because it is the
only way you will ever see her again.*

Masood eyes him and then agrees:

Agreed.

As Farzad nods, satisfied, Masood asks:

*You ever wonder why the Creator, after going to all the
trouble to create us, would want us to martyr ourselves just to
prove we're His creations?*

Farzad gets a worried look:

You should not speak like that.

Why not?

Just don't!

As Kraig, Emily and Brody move through mountain terrain,
angling back to where they think Chance might be, Brody reacts
to his tracking device:

Whoa!

They stop short. Kraig instantly turns:

What?

Looks like...he's headed back our way?

Brody moves the device so that it can detect the direction,
confirming the reading:

He's definitely heading this way.

Brody looks to Kraig:

But why?

I know why.

Kraig and Brody both look to her:
For the girl.

Hiking back to Zerak's farm, Chance and Farzad draw near enough to see the destroyed hut, ringed by cratered, blackened earth. Chance blanches and starts running towards it. So Farzad starts running, too.

As Chance runs up to see the scorched ground left by the hellfire missile, worried that all were killed, he hears something move and turns to see Tariq step from the remaining hut.
Tariq instantly recognizes Chance and pulls out his knife:
You did this. You brought this upon us. Didn't you?
No.
Yes. You did!
Tariq suddenly charges at Chance, wielding the knife.
Chance deflects his momentum by stepping aside, but Tariq manages to nevertheless cut him as he tumbles past.
As Tariq scrambles back to his feet, ready for more, a shot explodes into the ground by his feet.
Tariq is shocked at the sight of Farzad running up:
Stop or I will shoot you!
Tariq, his eyes burning, looks for a moment as he might prefer death to stopping his attack on Masood. But he finally relents:
As you can see, the Americans have already taken all we have. And now you protect their spies?
Farzad, remembering his promise to Masood, pretends to take an interest in Tariq's assertion. As Farzad draws him into conversation, distracting Tariq with questions, Masood moves off in a hurried search for Nadjia.

Moving out into the orchard, he finds her collecting firewood. As he hurries forward, she looks up at him blankly and then goes back to her work as if he wasn't even there.
Nadjia, it's me. Masood.
She looks up again, only now vaguely recognizing him:
What happened?
My father, my brother...

The look in her eyes completes her words, drawing tears to Masood's eyes:

I am so sorry.

As tears well up in her eyes, she collapses – and he grabs her to keep her from falling – causing her head scarf to loosen, revealing that her ear has been shorn off, covered by still-bloody cloth bandage.

Masood's eyes burn:

Tariq?

She nods, and he strains hard not to kill Tariq then and there. But he knows he has only a little time:

I will come back for you. Do you understand? I will come back and get you. And we will leave here together. I promise. All right?

He then retreats, moving back to Farzad, avoiding eye contact with Tariq.

Farzad bids good-bye to Tariq, promising future assistance, and then moves to catch up with Masood, confused:

So?

Masood keeps walking.

Was she all right?

...She will be.

Farzad senses something's up, but lets it go as they move on, heading back the way they came.

Above them, Kraig, peering through his scope, sees Masood hiking back into the mountains with Farzad:

We take him back at the pass.

Emily and Brody nod, ready to get this finally done, and move out to intercept him, while on another slope, Price takes in Masood's progress with a very different agenda:

Well, hello.

Price turns to his lieutenant:

Remember that Hadj Kraig let go free? Tell Command we have a confirmed ID on a Taliban unit, so 'bring the bang.'

As they hike on, Masood suddenly slows and looks around for a place to take a piss. He signals Farzad and moves to it.

A moment later, Farzad joins him, chuckling:

I didn't have to until you did.

As they relieve themselves, momentarily relaxing, a huge explosion suddenly sends them flying as a Hellfire missile lays waste where they were just walking.

Masood tumbles to the ground, dazed, reeling, suddenly seeing more images of himself as a young man battling the flames of a burning car in which a woman – his mother he now realizes – is trapped.

As he struggles back to his feet to save her, the car explodes into flames, instantly consuming all. As Masood – Chance – crumples back to his knees in anguish, he comes to again to find himself face down in Afghan dirt. Unable to move, he lays there, his ears ringing, his eyes burning, his head pounding as a small, quiet thought circles his mind:

I love my country. I believe in my country. I would die for my country...I just don't know which country is my country.

He then hears a distant voice yelling, and looks up to see Farzad, bloodied, yelling down at him in Pashtu, as if over a great distance.

But Chance cannot understand Farzad as he continues to yell at him in Pashtu, warning:

Hurry. Americans!

Farzad pulls Chance up and drags him away as Kraig, enraged by yet another unexpected missile strike, grabs the Satcom receiver:

This is Pride Five. Do you read, over!
We read you, pride five. Over.
Hold fire. Do you read? Hold fire, over!

Price and his lieutenant are meanwhile making their way down to the missile's kill zone, moving precisely, point to point, only to realize the missile must have missed:

So where are they?

His lieutenant shakes his head as Price looks around, snarling at defeat:

Goddamnit, we had 'em!

Price then looks up at the skies:

On a silver platter, goddamnit!

He then looks back at his lieutenant:

They can't have gone far.

His lieutenant replies soberly:

No, but now every goat-herder with a pea-shooter will be coming for us.

Price knows he's right, and they retreat back into the mountains with Price grumbling:

On a silver, fuckin' platter!

Kraig, scanning the terrain with his rifle scope, sees Farzad helping Chance escape:

He's alive!

He grabs the Satcom again:

This is Pride Five, request prior confirmation of all targets within our operating area, over.

Copy that, Pride Five, but we did get ground confirmation. Over.

Brody scowls as Kraig shakes his head, incredulous. They know only too well who gave that confirmation. He takes up the Satcom, about to give them what-for, but then reconsiders and says:

This time, you get it from me, or you don't engage target, do you read, over.

Copy that Pride Five, over.

Kraig looks at Emily:

This isn't how it's supposed to be. Or how it was supposed to go.

He then looks to Brody, who eyes him back, sensing a sea-change in his Captain:

What are ya thinking?

I'm thinking we not only extract him, but we e-vac him the hell out of here.

Brody considers:

Without getting clearance first?

If we ask for what, we might not get it.

But if we don't ask for it, we'll catch hell from Command.

No doubt.

Brody shrugs, reciting the obvious:

Our tour's almost over, ya know.

Kraig knows this only too well:

I'll understand if you need to take a pass.

Emily, feeling the weight behind their words, still doesn't understand what they're referring to, so she looks to Kraig:

Meaning?

Meaning we would all be going against orders if we e-vac'd him out without clearance. So the only question is...

He looks to Emily:

You okay with that?

Emily has to smile, bemused:

I am so okay with it.

Kraig then looks back at Brody, posing the same, now implicit question. Brody takes a moment to consider, but then shrugs:

Ah what the hell. Let's blow this pop stand.

Across the pass, Chance is lying on the ground, still dazed as Farzad tries to make him comfortable, reassuring him in Pashtu. Chance eyes Farzad, unable to understand him until Farzad uses the name 'Nadjia', at which Chance rallies:

Nadjia?

Chance struggles up, his memory nudged:

Nadjia?

Farzad replies in Pashtu, but all Chance can think of now is Nadjia, and, regaining his feet, he starts off, angling back to Zerak's orchard.

Farzad watches after him, conflicted, not sure if he should stay with the man who saved his life, or let him go his way and rejoin his brothers in arms.

After a moment's thought, Farzad retreats into the night, heading back to the Taliban camp...

On another slope, Kraig, Brody and Emily prepare to make their move, tracking Chance's movements:

He's on the move. Southbound.

Kraig smiles:

Heading right back for the girl.

Moving in the dark, Chance navigates in the moonlight, making his way through the spot where Kraig and company originally deposited him. From there he can see the remaining hut, so he quickens his pace.

When he arrives he moves quietly past the rubble of the first hut, past the last few remaining goats, to the remaining hut.

Easing alongside its wall, he gingerly rises up to peek inside its window to see Nadjia, asleep, and Tariq nearby, also asleep...

Sliding back out of view, wondering how he's going to wake Nadjia without waking Tariq, he hears someone stirring inside the hut.

So he backs into the shadows, holding his breath, only to see Nadjia stepping from the hut to head for the well.

Chance follows her, as quietly as he can, so quietly that only after she's had a cup of water and turns does she see him standing there.

She starts, but then recognizes him. She is filled with so much emotion that she lunges into his arms.

They hold each other in a squeezing, wordless embrace.

When she whispers something furtive to him in Pashtu, he realizes he doesn't understand her, either. So he tries to make her understand:

I came to take you away from this. Understand? Just like I promised!

She stares, unable to comprehend his English.

So he tries gesturing, improvising a sign language to reassure her:

We go. Now. You and me. Okay?

But she pulls back from him, alarmed, only to hear Tariq: *Nadjia!*

Her face fills with terror, and she motions for Chance to go. *I'll be back!*

He hides in the darkness as she hurries back into the hut.

As Chance retreats back into the mountains above the orchard, wondering what to do, he's suddenly driven to the ground from behind.

Only then does Kraig reveal himself, pinning Chance as Brody quickly handcuffs him. Chance struggles:

Wait!

They are all shocked at his English:

Let me go! You don't understand.

Kraig tests him:

What's your name?

Chance, breathing hard, says:

I don't know. But if you don't let me go, he's going to kill her!

Who is?

That guy down there!

Are you American or Afghan?

He eyes Kraig incredulously and then asks:

Does it matter?

The question hits Kraig like a shot, exposing, articulating, naming the pitched battle raging in Kraig's heart, and it takes him a moment to respond:

…What matters is that we got you, and we're getting you out of here.

No!

As Chance struggles against the cuffs, Kraig gives Brody a look:

Can we have that chopper now, please?

Brody immediately calls Command:

Command, this is Pride Five. Do you read, over?

Unable to free himself, Chance appeals to Kraig:

You must let me go!

The Satcom crackles to life:

Pride Five, this is Command. Over.

Kraig grabs the sitcom:

Pride Five requesting an immediate e-vac, over.

Roger that, Pride Five. Stand by for coordinates, over.

Chance kicks at Kraig, trying to get his attention:

I need ta try.

Kraig looks down at Chance, moved, but is still trying to pursue the only rationale he knows:

You'll fail.

Maybe. But ya still gotta let me go. And I don't want anybody ta come after me, either. I just need ya ta let me go!

Doesn't work like that, soldier.

Chance, perplexed by the word 'soldier', looks to Emily in anguish:

Can ya help me? Please?

As she hesitates, he looks back to Kraig:

Anything happens ta me, it's on me.

Kraig steels himself:

The Taliban is what will be on you, bro. And as for saving that woman? You two won't make it five feet together!

I can't leave here without her.

Kraig fires back:

Well you sure as hell can't leave here with her.

Chance eyes him, confused:

But...why not?

Because...

Kraig falters:

Because everything here's screwed up, that's why. Because far as I'm concerned, you shouldn't even be here, Soldier!

Chance again glances to Emily for help, but then appeals once more to Kraig:

But I am. And you're here, too. And I gotta try.

Not on my watch, pal.

Emily looks to Kraig:

Could we talk?

Kraig can guess what's coming, so only reluctantly does he move off with Emily, out of Chance's ear-shot. As a safe distance, Emily gives him a knowing look, but Kraig balks.

Are you kidding me?

He needs to try. Just like you would need to, just like I would need to.

He'll get himself killed, is what he'll do. Can you live with that?

Emily, coming to a new perception, hears herself say:

Whether I can or can't isn't the point.

Kraig eyes her incredulously:

So what, you're going to fry what's left of his brains? Send him back out there like a lamb to the slaughter?

Tears well in her eyes, and Kraig suddenly realizes this is as much about Emily's slain brother as it is about Chance.

All he knows, all he wants, all he needs is to save that girl.

Brody, meanwhile, waiting on the Satcom for Command's confirmation, grows impatient:

Oh come on, damn it.

As he begins to pace, preoccupied, he's suddenly hit over the head from behind.

He slumps forward, dazed to see Chance holding a rock behind him – which Chance then tosses aside to pull out Brody's knife and cut himself free.

Chance then quickly searches for Emily's laptop, finds it, and starts pasting the diodes onto his own head as Kraig and Emily, unaware, continue to debate:

Emily, listen to me: we have him. He's alive. We're alive. So we're leaving now, before anything more can go wrong. End of story.

Is that what you would want us to do, if you are in his shoes?

Kraig knows he wouldn't, but:

First Seally, then Riggs? None of this is what I would want. So I'm cutting our losses.

He marches back to find Brody staggering back to his feet:

What the hell?

Brody directs his attention to Emily's laptop.

Kraig sees the diodes and the program running, yet no sign of Chance. As it dawns on him what must have happened, Emily arrives, sees her laptop and quickly kneels to check. Then she looks up back up at Kraig, incredulous:

He tranced himself?

Kraig immediately hustles off into the dark in search of Chance while Emily moves to help Brody:

You all right?

Never better.

Moments later, Kraig hustles back into view:

I don't know why I'm chasing him when I know exactly where he's going.

Brody, knowing what comes next, shakes his head:

But the e-vac's already on its way. How do we extract him and make it back to the pick-up point?

Kraig checks his watch, his mind racing as he turns to Emily, formulating a precarious plan. And she senses it:

What are you thinking?

If what you said is true, and we e-vac out of here without Chance, Command will assume he's gone terminal, and order Price to take him out. Right?

Emily nods, realizing the unintended consequences of allowing Chance to stay.

But what if...

Emily and Brody wait:

What if you were to call Command now and say he's gone terminal. Then we'd get the orders to take him out, which would buy us time to extract him.

Brody's dubious:

But what if Command orders us to e-vac anyway, and leaves Chance to Price?

Kraig considers that alternative too:

Either way, I'm not going to leave him to Price, so...anybody got a better plan?

Emily and Brody trade a look, shaking their heads, at which Brody hands her the Satcom:

Tell 'em he's gone terminal, but that we have a read on his position.

An hour later and a mountain-slope away, Price listens to Command's reply over his Satcom:

Copy that. Eagle out.

Price turns to his lieutenant:

'Member that Hadj Kraig was protecting? Command wants him taken out.

'Bout time.

As they head out on their new mission, Price grins:

Don't ya love it when everything just falls into place?

Down range, Farzad, making his way back, hears a man call his name from the shadows, and turns to see Hakim stepping into view.

Hakim? What are you doing here?

A group of armed Taliban fighters emerge from the shadows to flank him:

We have returned for the blasphemer.

Farzad, realizing he too is now in danger because of his association with Masood, shifts course, and tries to prove his loyalty:

I know where he has gone. I will take you to him.

As a cosmos of stars mass in the black night sky above him, Chance hikes quickly over the rock mountain terrain, hurrying back to Zerak's farm.

Cresting a hill, he can see the remaining hut in the moonlight below.

Encouraged, he makes his way down the steep, rough slope as quietly as he can.

Descending to the hut by another slope, Brody picks up Chance's movements on his GPS, and points out his position to Kraig, who adjusts their angle of approach accordingly on the move.

Arriving on the plateau, Chance – Masood – works his way up to the hut and carefully peeks in through the window to see a silhouette in the shadows, motioning him around back.

So Masood ducks out of view and creeps around to the back of the hut, excited, ready to take Nadjia into his arms when Tariq suddenly charges from the shadows to tackle him to the ground, intent on gouging out Masood's eyes with a knife.

They tumble, rolling around in hand to hand combat as Tariq stabs at Masood's eyes just as Price and his lieutenant, now within a hundred yards, set up for a sniper shot, only to see the fight through his scope:

Oh come on! Don't tell me this sonofabitch gonna take him out before I do.

Price fires a round at the two of them as they roll around, but misses as Kraig and company, still unaware of Price, are running towards the plateau while Tariq manages to hit Masood with the butt of the knife, dazing him. He then quickly follows with two more vicious hits to Masood's head, knocking him.

Tariq then maneuvers Masood's head so that he can pluck out his eyes. And just as he angles his knife to begin the blunt surgery, a shot rings out, exploding through Tariq's left eye as the bullet passes through his head.

Tariq freezes a beat and then crumples to the ground as Price and the lieutenant, having just witnessed it, quickly pan their scopes to locate Nadjia, holding Tariq's Kalashnikov rifle, standing at the hut's door.

Price protests:

What the hell?

They then see Kraig and Brody quickly approaching the area, fanning out point to point, ready to take out Nadjia or anyone else if need be.

Price spits:

Oh for crying out loud, not this time, buddy. Not this time.

Price relocates Masood in his scope, and just as he lines up the kill shot, a barrage of semi-automatic weapons fire suddenly sprays the hut.

Kraig and Brody dive for cover as Hakim's band of fighters fire at them behind the trees of the orchard, pock-marking everything in sight with their fierce rounds of fire.

Nadjia dives back inside the hut, pinned down by the fire as Masood, coming to, stretches out on the ground as flat as he can to avoid the bullets screaming just over his head and body.

Price grimaces, more angry than afraid as he's forced to abandon his kill shot:

Goddamnit!

He and his lieutenant then hustle to their feet and move to locate where the Taliban are hiding.

Kraig and Brody meanwhile are crouching behind the hut, returning fire as they can, but taking on far more fire-power than they can return. Kraig yells:

We gotta move from here.

A moment later, using the hut for cover they back away into the dark, then circle back around, angling for the orchard, hoping to surprise the Taliban from their flank.

Price, using his scope, locates the Taliban's position in the orchard, and takes out the Satcom:

Eagle Two, do you read.

We read you, Eagle Two.

Request immediate strike on my mark. Can you deliver, over?

Roger that, Eagle Two. Bird moving into position. Stand by, over.

As the drone's infrared camera picks up the heat signatures of the fire-fight below, Price's Satcom buzzes back to life:

Roger, Eagle two. Bird ready and waiting for your mark, over.

Price, sensing his moment has finally arrived, un-clips his soflam laser and beams it at the orchard, just as his lieutenant spots Kraig and Brody sneaking into the orchard.

Wait. 'Are those our guys?

Price makes short-shrift of trying to locate what his lieutenant is seeing, and dismisses it:

Maybe, maybe not. But if the Hadj make it out of that orchard, we're all dead.

As the lieutenant looks on conflicted, Price barks into the Satcom:

Bring the bang, over!

Just then, Kraig and Brody, entering the orchard, engage the Taliban, firing into their lines from their flank just as a Hellfire missile streaks down from the night sky to explode in the orchard, obliterating men and trees in a fiery burst that boils up in the darkness, igniting a frenzied fire storm through the trees.

Price and the lieutenant then hustle towards the hut.

Masood and Nadjia, realizing the gunfire has stopped, look up from their positions to see the orchard burning.

Masood pulls himself up and hurries to hold Nadjia. He then lifts her to her feet, eager to get her as far from here as he can. But then they hear:

Halt!

They turn, startled to see Price and his lieutenant, rifles
raised, outside the hut.

Price indicates they should step out, and they do:

Anybody speak English?

Chance and Nadjia stare at him, holding each other, scared
as Price smirks with disgust:

No? That's what I thought.

Masood, in Pashtu, demands:

Leave us alone!

Price chuckles, his suspicions confirmed:

*I don't know what the dude just said, but I hope it was real
good, cause it's gonna be the last thing he says.*

Price raises his rifle, indicating Masood and Nadjia should
move apart:

Step away from her, bro. Now!

Masood understands what Price wants him to do, but he
refuses, holding Nadjia even closer.

*Oh look, gotta regular Romeo and Juliet, huh? Okey-dokey.
If that's the way ya want it.*

Price, relishing this challenge to his armed authority, raises
his rifle, willing to take them both, only to hear:

No!

Price, startled, quickly pivots to see Kraig, covered in dirt,
staggering into view, followed by Brody.

Price's eyes narrow, not pleased to see Kraig, but he covers
his disappointment with a smirk:

*Well if it isn't Dudley DoRight. Sorry, pal, but this time, I
got my orders.*

Kraig raises his rifle and trains it at Price:

I said no.

The lieutenant raises his rifle, angling it at Kraig,
prompting Brody to raise his rifle and point it at the lieutenant.

Price grins, enjoying the mutual checkmate:

Don't make me do what I gotta do, Kraig.

*You mean fuck everything up even more than you already
have?*

Price shakes his head, bemused:

*What you don't seem to get, Kraig, is there's us, the good
guys, and there's them, the bad guys. That's how it is, and that's*

how it'll always be. And if you don't know which side you're on, you're like...royally screwed, dude.

Kraig smiles, marveling ironically:

Your lack of situational awareness, Price, is epic.

My 'situational awareness'? It's candy-ass pansies like you that are the problem, Kraig. You and your merry band of eunuchs who don't have the balls to do what needs to be done. You're the reason we lost this goddamn war! But not tonight. So back off!

Kraig calmly cocks his gun, raising the ante.

Price smiles, welcoming the stakes:

That is supposed to be a threat, dude?

I'm not threatening you, Price. I'm just confirming what will happen if you don't back off.

Price grins and then gestures at Chance to his lieutenant, picking the order of shots:

I take him.

Price then indicates Kraig:

He takes me out just as you take him.

They then hear:

How about I take you out first?

Surprised, they all turn to see Emily walking right into the middle of their standoff, pointing one of the fallen Taliban's rifles at Price as she interposes herself between Price and Chance:

Did you hear me? Or were you too busy calling in Hellfire missiles on your own men?

Price sneers:

That wasn't our fault.

Emily nods at Kraig:

Then maybe he'll forgive you. But in the meantime, Command wants these two – she indicates Chance and Nadjia – *e-vac'd out of here now, so if you don't mind?*

Emily, Kraig and Brody, keeping their guns poised at Price and the lieutenant, start backing away as Price, beginning to boil, looks on, on the brink of firing...

But the more distance they put between themselves and Price, he slowly but surely backs down, convinced they would have all died...

Kraig, Emily, Brody, Chance and Nadjia move out to an open area as a chopper descends from above.

A minute later, they climb into the Chopper's cargo bay, Nadjia hesitating, but Chance reassuring her.

As they lift away, Chance – Masood – holds Nadjia's hand as Kraig looks on:

Corporal Chance?

Masood doesn't respond.

Kraig looks to Emily, so she tries:

Masood?

Still no response.

Gavin? Gavin Chance?

Nadjia looks up, confused, but Chance doesn't seem to recognize any of his names. Kraig looks once more to Emily as she muses:

He's not any of them now.

Brody hears that and looks up, concerned.

So who is he?

Emily sees how he's holding Nadjia:

He's the guy taking care of her. That's the only story he knows now.

Brody sobers:

Will he ever...?

Hopefully. In time. With a great deal of help.

Kraig considers, and looks back at Chance:

Hey, Bro?

Chance looks up, sensing he's being spoken to:

Everything's going to be okay.

Their eyes share a look, Chance seeming to sense Kraig's intent even if he can't understand its exact meaning, as Emily regards Nadjia:

She'll need time too. But at least they'll have each other.

Kraig takes that in, feeling the years of service, training, study, sleep deprivation, combat, idealism and shattered realities wash over his face, releasing finally into a small smile of recognition:

Your career's over, you know.

Emily nods, resigned, and then notes:

So's yours.

He weighs that without worry or regret.

Well, least we'll have each other.

Without looking at him, Emily seems to go into herself for a moment and then resurfaces with a small, quiet smile:

Finally, something we can agree on.

As their eyes find each other, they begin to feel freed, freed from the isolating beliefs and lonely certitudes, freed from their constricted roles and temporal assumptions. In letting go of their stories, their reasons and reductions, a weight drops away from them like the dark earth below, discovering as it does a peace not in flight or escape, but in the recognition and release from all the illusions and delusions that ever kept them apart.

~*~

Raised in Los Angeles, Darryl Sollerh's recent works include
"EDDY FALLS", "ALIBIS OF THE HEART", a Readers'
Favorite Book Award FINALIST, "TRANCER", "MINDFALL"
and "COWBOY AND INDIAN", a Readers' Favorite SILVER
MEDAL Award winner. All are available in print, and on Kindle,
iPad, Nook and eReaders everywhere. For more, visit
www.DarrylSollerh.com

~*~

For Imran

~*~

www.ingramcontent.com/pod-product-compliance
Lightning Source LLC
Chambersburg PA
CBHW020637130626
46552CB00003B/1280